THESE BOOTS ARE MADE FOR WITCHING

T.M. CROMER

Wicked Witchmas Copyright © 2024 T.M. Cromer

ISBN: 978-1-956941-42-5 (EPUB)
ISBN: 978-1-956941-57-9 (PAPERBACK)

All rights reserved. No part of this publication may be reproduced, distributed, or transmitted in any form or by any means, including photocopying, recording, or other electronic or mechanical methods, without the prior written permission of the publisher, except in the case of brief quotations embodied in critical reviews and certain other noncommercial uses permitted by copyright law.

NO AI TRAINING: Without in any way limiting the author's [and publisher's] exclusive rights under copyright, any use of this publication to "train" generative artificial intelligence (AI) technologies to generate text is expressly prohibited. The author reserves all rights to license uses of this work for generative AI training and development of machine learning language models.

This is a work of fiction. Names, characters, businesses, places, events, and incidents are either the products of the author's imagination or used in a fictitious manner. Any resemblance to actual persons, living or dead, or actual events is purely coincidental.

Deanna Chase,
This is as H-mark as I get.

Renee George,
Thanks for the body doubling and support. Your friendship is the gold standard.

CJ Obray,
Thanks for being a great sprinting buddy and checking in when I went "dark."

CHAPTER ONE

Tripp Nightshade.

Elara's heart beat painfully as she ducked into the alley beside the *Never Too Many* bookstore. Of *course* she'd run into him after clocking out for the day. That's how her luck worked. But why was she bothering to hide when Tripp had no clue she existed? Yeah, it was a question for a therapist.

Speaking of...

She checked her smartwatch. If she didn't gather the courage to leave this alley, she'd be late for her appointment with Dr. Cobb. Oh, what she wouldn't give for the ability to teleport like other witches were reported to have! As it was, she had no choice but to step onto the main thoroughfare and go about her business. Hopefully minus the flushed face and stutter she seemed to develop around Tripp.

"You can do this, Elara," she muttered. "He's just a guy like any other."

But he wasn't.

He was Tripp Nightshade, the most beautiful man in existence. Long, wavy hair, dark as midnight, with eyes just a shade lighter.

They glowed with purpose and a power rumored to have been handed down from the Gods themselves. And oh, those rounded shoulders!

Pressing a hand to her chest, she sighed.

Yes, those glorious, *glorious* shoulders. So muscular. So manly. So—

"Elara?"

She screamed. The sound was worthy of a slasher film, bringing Tripp running.

He gripped her upper arms. "Are you all right? What's wrong?"

Unable to answer, she fluttered a hand between them. She was pretty sure if she tried to speak, she'd choke on her tongue—mainly from the desire to taste *his* in *her* mouth.

"Pass the salami," she blurted.

"Excuse me?" His furrowed brows shot to his hairline, changing his look from concerned to comical. "What did you say?"

Think fast, Elara. Think fast.

But she couldn't. Around him, her brain matter ran slower than sludge traveling uphill.

Over boulders.

During a torrential downpour.

With an awkward squawk, she shoved him and ran for the street. The sound of her sneakers pounding the pavement was drowned by the deafening thud of her pulse in her ears. That thrumming was also why she missed hearing Tripp come up behind her.

His grip on her bicep halted her progress, but the high-speed momentum of her spectacularly spasmatic escape propelled her around and straight into his arms. Her eyes rolled back in delight at the contact of her breasts pressed to his muscled chest.

Or maybe it was from the not-so-pleasurable contact of her nose hitting his rock-hard pec.

She had two entire seconds to register his clean, crisp, albeit woodsy, scent before the pain struck and her eyes teared up. Swearing like a boozy old lush suffering a five-day drought, Elara spat out every word in her repertoire and created a few more to boot. In the seconds before she tipped her head back and pinched her nose, she glanced at him. Poor Tripp appeared horrified—and somewhat traumatized—by the entire experience.

Well, he wasn't the only one!

"Did you break it?"

She couldn't be one hundred percent positive, but she thought she detected laughter in his voice. Narrowing her watery eyes, she wiggled the bridge of her nose. "I don't think so, but you need to register that body as a lethal weapon. You can't go around crashing into unsuspecting females, potentially rearranging their facial features, all because your... your..."

Her brain went as mushy as a toasted marshmallow as she stared at his sculpted chest beneath the buttery soft material of his thin sweater. This last part she knew because her left hand had a mind of its own and was brushing the heavenly texture.

He cleared his throat.

She slammed her lids closed. "I don't suppose you have a spell in your family's grimoire that can erase this entire incident from our memories, do you?"

"Maybe." There was definitely laughter in his voice this time.

"Will you use it for me?"

"Nope."

She sighed her disappointment. "Yeah, I didn't think so. Later."

His wicked chuckle filled her ears as she turned to go.

"Oh, Elara."

Did she dare turn around? The temptation to bask in the light of his splendor was great, but she remained with her back to him.

"You forgot the, uh, *salami.*"

"Kill me now," she muttered.

"What was that?"

"*Nothing!*"

. . .

As Elara hurried away, ash-blonde hair flying behind her in the December breeze, Tripp bit his lip to hold back his laughter. But the moment she turned the corner, he sobered.

The day turned exceedingly duller. Yes, he'd known about her crush on him for some time, and the wicked devil inside him took every opportunity to fluster her. One could say that causing her acute discomfort had become his favorite pastime.

Tripp was a demigod, although few recognized it. He wasn't being arrogant to believe most of the women in Witchmere wanted him. Sex appeal came part and parcel with his brand of supreme magic. Hell, he practically had to fight people off with a stick, as annoying as it was.

But Elara was different.

She was quirky and cute. Her inability to look higher than his chin was charming, not irritating. And Tripp absolutely loved how she'd rather run away than attempt to seduce him. Call him twisted, but her shyness was an absolute turn-on. With one nervous glance from those large china-blue eyes, she slayed him.

"You should put that girl out of her misery. Just bend her over the barrel and show her the fifty states already. Maybe then she'd stop hiding in alleyways."

He choked back another laugh as he shifted toward the employee entrance of the bookstore.

The gruff, smokes-two-packs-a-day voice hadn't surprised him. He'd sensed the business owner's presence the instant she stepped into the alley. He was, however, somewhat shocked she'd addressed him directly. Unless Florence Rose Shaw was calling to inform him that his book order was ready, she refused to have anything to do with him.

Fear caused responses like hers.

Fear of the Ancient World power he possessed.

Not that he blamed her. If he wasn't the one wielding it, he'd be wary, too.

"You surprise me, Flo." As he strolled toward her, he shoved his fists deep in his slacks pockets. Long ago, he'd discovered it made others more comfortable if his hands were sheathed. Effortless abilities, such as his, made people sweat. "I thought you liked the girl. Surely you wouldn't want her in the hands of an uncaring immortal."

"I do like her, but watching her avoid you is downright painful. The poor chit."

Tripp grinned. "She does it well."

A fond smile cracked Florence's wrinkled face. "The gel's crafty."

"Yes." He half turned, closing his eyes to get a location of where Elara had gone. Zeroing in, he frowned. "Why is she meeting Harrison Cobb?"

"Is she?" Light flared as Florence touched a fingertip to her unlit, home-rolled cigarette.

"You know she is. It's the reason she's not at work right now."

After a long drag, she blew smoke into the air from the corner of her mouth, away from him, and shrugged.

Instead of becoming irritated by her evasiveness, he embraced the warmth of her caring for Elara, basking in the love the older woman felt for her *supposed* employee.

"Have you told her who you are yet?" he asked softly. "Does she know you're her grandmother?"

"No." Abruptly, she dashed the cigarette against the brick and stuffed the unused section into her cardigan. "She'll despise me if I tell her."

He frowned as he considered her problem. As someone who'd been around centuries, he was well aware of the standard issues mortals faced—even witchy ones. Familial relationships were the worst.

And didn't he know it!

As the son of a goddess, he had it worse than most. Longer, too. Dearest Mommy expected him home whenever she deemed it necessary to summon him, but he was a moving target, never staying in one place long enough for her minions to find him. Eventually, she would, but Tripp enjoyed the freedom while he could.

"You're wrong," he told Florence. "She's been looking for a connection since she and Payton arrived in Witchmere, and who better to connect with than the one person who owns the bookstore she adores so much?"

"She'll inherit when I'm gone."

His senses consumed her underlying insecurities, feasting on them to lessen her worry. "Tell her, Flo. She'll understand."

"What did you just do, boy?"

"Boy? That's like calling *me* a cuddly puppy." The voice was raspy and deep, emanating from the shadows next to the dumpster.

Tripp chuckled. "Nicely done, Sanderson."

"Thanks. I try." Bodhan Sanderson stepped into the light and bowed his shaggy, light-brown head.

"I know."

For two and a half years, he'd used his wolf-shifter skills to best Tripp in an ongoing game of surprise attack, seldom gaining the advantage. Tripp's unfailing ability to sense magic acted as his early warning system. On rare occasions, like this one where he was distracted, Bodhan had succeeded in getting within ten feet of him, but no closer.

"Don't you have woods to wander, cuddly puppy?" Florence shot him an irritated scowl. "And whatever you overheard with those obnoxiously large ears of yours had better remain a secret, hear?"

Thoroughly offended and made self-conscious by her comment, Bodhan reached a hand up as if to test the size of his ear.

Tripp snorted. Florence had a way of putting the townsfolk in their place, and he loved it.

"You're one to laugh, Tripp Nightshade. Hiding out from deities like a recalcitrant schoolboy."

His blood froze. How did she know?

With a shake of her head and a warning glare for both, she hurried through her shop door.

Bodhan winced. "She didn't have to slam the bolt so hard. It's not like we were chasing her or anything."

"Don't feel insulted. That was for my benefit." Tripp shrugged. "She likely sprinkled wolfsbane along the door openings and is burning sage by now."

"She might sell more books if she were a bit friendlier," Bodhan hollered in the direction of the door.

"Go to the devil, cuddly puppy!" Florence shouted back.

"Do you think she knows she's horrid?" he asked Tripp.

"She's not." Although she truly was, Tripp needed to get on her good side to find out what she knew about him, and the only way to do that was to convince her that he was a decent guy. He met Bodhan's disbelieving gaze and shrugged. "You just have to get to know her."

He was lucky lightning didn't strike him dead.

Bodhan laughed, damn him.

"So Elara and Payton are her granddaughters. I didn't see that one coming."

"For a small town, this place has more drama than a television soap opera." Tripp grimaced. "I'd appreciate it if you'd keep that under your hat, Sanderson. If you don't, I'll have to give in to Avery Barker's seduction, and we both know very well how you feel about her."

"You're evil," Bodhan growled. And although there would be no contest in a fight like theirs, the wolf-like sound raised the hair on Tripp's neck.

"All you had to do was ask," his friend grumbled.

"Apologies. I was raised to trust no one, and old habits die hard." Tripp felt like a Grade-A prick for his threat. The other man had given him no reason to believe he'd spread rumors. In fact, Bodhan was as close-mouthed as they came.

Yet Tripp wasn't lying when he said he was raised to trust no one. Gods were notorious for their games and playing one person against another. If he could settle in a place long enough, perhaps he'd make better connections. Not likely, though, because his time was limited here, just as it was everywhere. But a demigod could dream of putting down roots, right?

CHAPTER TWO

Tripp Nightshade.

Elara had waxed on about him ad nauseam during her appointment, to the point Harrison Cobb dozed off. And what did that say about her obsession? More importantly, what did it say about *her*? If she couldn't keep her therapist engaged, how could she keep someone like Tripp from snoozing?

"My apologies, Elara," Harrison said, wiping saliva from the side of his mouth and blinking away his embarrassment. "It wasn't you. I—"

"No, it's okay, Dr. Cobb." She smiled weakly. "I may have gotten carried away." And why wouldn't she? Tripp was heavenly. Still, the world didn't need to know about her pathetic crush. She prayed Harrison wouldn't retell the story of this appointment to his therapist cronies at their next shrink convention.

"Elara." His voice was kind and caring, but she imagined he utilized that tone with everyone.

"You don't have to say it."

And he didn't. Her self-doubt routine was old, even to her. What she wouldn't give for something to make her interesting, though. Something to make her sexy and untamed, perhaps a little wicked, so she'd be worthy in Tripp's eyes. Many would tell her a man wasn't worth it if she had to work so hard to keep his attention, and they were right.

Mostly.

The exception: *Tripp*.

"I'll see you next month, Doc."

Or not.

What did she really have to complain about anyway? Many, many people had it worse in the world. So what if she was suffering unrequited love? So what if her parents were deadbeats who took off without a word, and the only person to care about her was her wild-child sister, who only ever thought of herself? She had a job—granted, one that didn't pay well—and a roof over her head, right?

Elara sailed out the door before rebooking. The office manager had billed her before the appointment and would no doubt call by next week to book a follow-up. But just maybe, she wouldn't answer. After her embarrassing moment in the alley, what was the point? She needed to leave Witchmere and start over somewhere no one knew her. Somewhere Tripp Nightshade wasn't. If she didn't, she'd continue to make a cake of herself and never find a life partner. How could she when she was consumed by thoughts of a relationship with a man she could never have?

She made it to the main road with relative ease, but the rest of her day went straight to hell. It didn't pass Go or collect two hundred dollars.

Across the street from Dr. Cobb's office building, Tripp was embracing another woman.

Elara's stomach bottomed out, and her chest literally ached, feeling uncomfortably like a heart attack. Had someone offered her a million dollars, right then and there, to control her facial expression, she'd be unable to manage it. So when Tripp glanced her way, her dismay was on full display. For a fleeting moment, their gazes locked, and he appeared regretful.

Yep. She had to leave this place. *Pronto!*

Doing what she'd done hundreds of times in hundreds of situations, she smiled tightly and turned away, hurrying down the sidewalk toward her apartment building. Thank goodness Witchmere was a small town, and everything was within walking distance because it only took her three minutes and fifteen seconds to reach her door. By three minutes and seventeen seconds, she had it unlocked, and by three minutes and twenty-five seconds, she was face down on her bed, giving into self-pity.

"Meow." The sound was a raspy mix of hoarseness and harshness, as if her cat were struggling to produce it.

"Please, leave me alone, Hex. I don't want you to see me this way."

She'd have sworn she heard him harumph right before repeatedly nudging her, thereby forcing her to roll onto her side. He settled against her abdomen in the C her curled-up body made. Giving him a rub behind the ear, as was his due, she sniffed.

"What part of 'leave me alone' didn't you get, you pushy thing?"

If a feline could roll its eyes, Sir Hex-a-lot would've. Hell, Elara wasn't positive he didn't. The beast butted her hand and twisted to expose his underside.

"I'm not falling for this one. Rubbing your belly will end in me being bitten," she replied.

He cracked one eyelid and glared with his eerie emerald eye, made brighter by the black of his shiny coat.

"Fine. But if you bite me, you're only getting kibble for the next week. No snacky snacks."

"Meow."

Knocking sounded from the other room, and Elara held her breath as she considered her options. Her sister had a key, and if she'd forgotten it, she could unlock the door using magic. Odds were she wouldn't knock. It wasn't as if she had friends, and no one else ever bothered to come by.

Her traitorous heart perked up, sure it was Tripp. But Elara shut that shit down. Two factors were fighting against her hope. One, he didn't know where she lived. Two, he had another to occupy his time. Rowen Sanderson. She was one of many townies and was beautiful in every way. It didn't hurt that she had her shit together, unlike her.

"Elara."

She sat up so fast and straight that had anyone seen her, they'd believe a cattle prod was inserted up her rump.

"Tripp," she whispered in horror to Hex. "What do I do?"

"You open the door," Tripp called.

She frowned.

How the hell had he heard her?

Shaking her head, she flopped onto her back. She was dreaming. She had to be.

"Elara, open the damned door."

"Go away," she hollered. "I'm napping!"

Her door flew back on its hinges. From her spot on the bed, she watched in stunned amazement as Tripp's curious gaze surveyed his surroundings before it landed on her. She launched herself from the bed as if her ass caught fire, causing Hex to hiss his irritation. And, like any annoyed feline looking to show his displeasure, he hiked a leg and began licking his balls.

"Manners, Hex," she reminded him.

The cat ignored her.

"Rude," she muttered.

When she looked up, it was to find Tripp leaning against the doorjamb of her bedroom, arms crossed and a wide grin on his perfect face. Anger brewed inside her belly like a boiling cauldron, ready to bubble over.

Of all the arrogant, self-assured Neanderthals!

"Why the blue blazes did you break into my place, and why shouldn't I call Dailey Cobb to come arrest your gorgeous ass?" She barely managed to stop her jaw from dropping. Why the hell did every thought pop out of her mouth around him?

His dark eyes gleamed with unholy amusement, but he merely watched her.

"Don't think I won't you... you... you scoundrel!"

Proud of herself, she squared her shoulders and glared.

His black brows shot up, but he remained silent, thereby causing her meltdown. Why did no one listen to her? Where was the respect she tried hard to earn?

"You're a good-for-nothing gigolo, determined to leave a trail of broken hearts in your wake with your wide, glorious shoulders and devil-may-care attitude. Does Rowen know you're here? Probably not!"

As per usual, Tripp allowed Elara to ramble on and dig herself in deeper. During her sputtering stand, she used the heels of her hands to swipe at the tears on her fresh, makeup-less face. The sight of her upset caused his stomach to sour. He'd been on his way to speak with her when Rowan thought flinging herself in his arms would be a good idea. Understanding her aim was to annoy Harrison, who happened to be glancing out the window at that precise moment, Tripp did nothing to stop her.

Unfortunately, he hadn't planned for Elara to leave the building right then. Hell, she'd had another fifteen minutes left of her appointment. How was he to know she'd chosen that exact second to walk out the door? He'd tried to tell himself he wasn't doing anything wrong by allowing Rowan to play her games, but Elara's feelings had been caught in the crossfire, and her expression was like a fucking gut punch.

"I'm sorry," he said, unfolding his arms and straightening.

"You should be. You can't just go around breaking into women's apartments. No wonder half the town thinks you're—"

"No, Elara. I'm not sorry for storming the gates. I'm sorry about Rowen."

Her skin flushed the shade of a turnip, and she presented her back, giving a little shrug in the process. "Why should I care?"

Why, indeed? But she did, and oddly, he did, too.

"You shouldn't," he told her, and it was the absolute truth. She would only get her heart broken when he left. And he *would* leave. He'd be forced to when his mother eventually discovered his location. Demigods could keep a low profile if they kept their abilities under wraps, but they still produced a magical signature, and a skilled tracker could—and would—find them.

"Well, I don't," she snapped, whirling to face him. "And if you don't mind, I'd like you to leave. I have things to do."

The devil on his shoulder held more influence than any angel could, and Tripp couldn't let her comment go unchallenged. He stepped toward her.

"Such as?"

Like a goldfish trapped in a bowl, her mouth opened and closed rhythmically.

"Well?" he taunted softly when there were fewer than three inches between them.

He could smell the peppermint on her huffing breath, and for the first time in his life, he decided he didn't hate the cooling scent. His desire to taste it, to taste *her*, was driving him to behave recklessly. If he kissed her, things would never be the same for either of them.

"Cat got your tongue, sweetheart?" his inner devil whispered into the shell of her ear.

The shock of her fingers weaving through his hair was a live wire through his system, and his body woke from its semi-slumbering state. Magic crackled around them as she tugged his head back and stared into his eyes.

Hers were large and wary, like a doe encountering a wolf. But deep in their recesses, he saw the answering spark of the inferno she had just ignited. Naturally red, plump lips parted, beckoning and urging him to throw caution to the wind. And when the tip of her pink tongue swept the opening, adding the sheerest hint of glistening moisture, he groaned.

Their bodies, needing no instruction, gravitated together, and the feel of her firm breasts pressed to his chest sent blood shooting to his dick. Tripp hadn't had an instantaneous reaction like this in decades, and the building hard-on pressing against the wall of her soft belly was about to get him into serious trouble.

Her focus dropped to his mouth, and she released a kitten-like mewl.

He was lost.

With nothing left but the all-consuming need to touch, to kiss, to savor her peppermint flavor, he did.

The instant his tongue met hers, the room darkened. Beyond the window, a flickering lightning flash was followed by a resounding thunderous boom. It shook the building before the skies opened, and a sideways sweeping downpour began.

Still, their kiss continued. Her hands burrowed under his cashmere sweater, and her fingertips dug into his lat muscles as if she held on for dear life. He, in turn, cradled her face between his large palms. The feel of her silky skin was everything he'd imagined on those nights when he gave himself leave to fantasize about touching her.

With senses thoroughly flooded by the raging elements and Elara's unexpected passion, Tripp jerked backward, breathing hard. Those sparkling eyes, cheeks flushed a becoming shade of rose, and kiss-swollen lips a deep crimson made her look like a goddess come to life. The thudding of his pulse nearly drowned out the pounding rain.

"Who the hell knew you could kiss like that?" He didn't recognize the hoarse voice as his own.

Eyes as wide as saucers, she used her fingertips to caress her mouth. That light, teasing touch almost did him in. Either he needed to escape to regroup, or he should sweep her into bed and never leave it again.

"I gotta go," he muttered. But he was reluctant to teleport away, especially when disappointment shone in her expressive peepers.

"I have to," he insisted.

Because if he didn't, the storm they'd inadvertently caused might become a typhoon of epic proportions and wipe Witchmere off the map. But he didn't dare tell her that. It would never do to let another know the power they could evoke in him.

CHAPTER THREE

Tripp Nightshade.

Such a ridiculous name!

Brelenia sighed her irritation.

"We've found him, my queen."

"Excellent. Where?" She held back her smile of satisfaction.

"A small town in the Pacific Northwest."

"And?"

"It appears he's formed an attachment."

Yes. She'd felt the moment he kissed his potential mate. They *all* did here on the island of Messia, where their family of gods and goddesses dwelled. Her wayward son had made a monumental mistake today. So much so, the repercussion could be felt in the rumbling vibration of the ground beneath her feet.

Having it confirmed, she waved away the handmaiden. "You may go, Eloisa. Thank you."

After the young woman bowed and backed away, Brelenia allowed herself a triumphant smile.

"You've met your downfall, Enguerrand," she said aloud as if her son were in the room. "Watching you navigate the maelstrom will be entertaining to the extreme."

She almost felt sorry for him, for what was to come.
Almost.

Brelenia crossed to her wardrobe and swept aside the gossamer curtains. The room was larger than her bedchamber and contained clothing she'd favored throughout the centuries, from creation day to the present. As one inclined to prefer tidy surroundings, she maintained staff who were as organized as she was and cared for her precious treasures as if they were their own.

But the one thing Brelenia never shared, the prized possession she'd kept hidden, was a unique pair of footwear, able to adapt to the person wearing them. They might sometimes appear as sandals, at other times as clogs, or even as boots. When possessed by the unworthy, they created catastrophic chaos. But a chosen one could wield their magic, given the proper incentive.

As their first owner, she ultimately found a partner in Enguerrand the Second. Their journey hadn't been without its trials, as were all deity-mortal relationships. However, they'd developed a deep, abiding love the bards wrote songs about and other couples coveted.

Enguerrand the Third, or Tripp, as he preferred to be called, was the first of their five offspring who refused to settle down. Like his father before him, her firstborn was stubborn to a fault and declined to accept direction. The boy would cut off his left arm if it meant spiting Brelenia. The foolish child believed he could hide from *her*.

Born of a drunken union between Cronus and the lesser goddess, Darana, Brelenia was the unknown half-sister of Zeus. Her birth had been hidden by necessity, as Cronus was fond of killing his children so they didn't overthrow him and reign supreme.

She had never desired the responsibility Zeus assumed when he defeated their father, and she was happy ruling her island for eternity as a relative unknown. Her job as ruler of hard-working, kind people who wished for peace above all things fulfilled her and kept her too busy to bother with war and the headaches it brought.

"What has you so deep in thought, my darling?"

She glanced up to see her lover. "What else?"

"Ah, Tripp." Eyes dancing, Rand smiled. The gesture was broad and engaging, causing her to sigh, much like she had when she was a mere girl and first saw him wield his wicked grin at another.

"If you knew, darling, why did you ask?"

"You like to say, 'He's stubborn like his father,' but it's *you* he takes after, Brel. How many centuries have you been trying to marry the poor boy off?"

"I've lost count."

His chuckle was felt to her toes, and she curled them in response. She tilted her head to let him lavish her neck with nibbling kisses.

"Our 'poor boy' is hopeless, Rand! His rebellion is delaying my job to see the rest of our children settled."

"There's no reason you can't see to their futures. Let Tripp run free, Brel. It's not causing any harm."

"Of course it is! Did you forget about the last disaster?"

"The Titanic?" At her nod, he frowned. "I keep telling you it was faulty ship design and an iceberg, darling."

"And I keep telling *you* it was because he tried to dodge the Fates. Those poor people might still be alive if it weren't for his obsessive need to avoid entanglement." Rand's snort annoyed her, and she sent him a sour look as she crossed the room. "Roll your eyes all you want. We both know the truth, and so does Enguerrand."

"For the love of Messia, Brelenia! Stop buying into this madness."

Hurt that he couldn't see her point of view, she shrugged and poured herself more wine from one of three carafes sitting on the sideboard. "Believe it or not, but his relationship woes have caused fifty percent of the world's natural disasters—and a good forty percent of the man-made ones."

"Look, I'll grant he was misguided during the French Revolution, but didn't he rectify it by encouraging Wellington to remain strong, leading to the capture of Napoleon?"

"Precisely my point! If he hadn't put ideas in the heads of those poor peasants, none of it would've happened."

"It would've happened anyway, Brel. The people were hungry, and their living conditions were abysmal." Rand approached and hugged her from behind. "Their monarch could've used your counsel in running their country." With a nod toward the balcony, he pointed out the group laughing in the courtyard. "Everyone is happy here because you've provided what they need. You're an excellent ruler of Messia. Tripp realizes that, too. He simply went about helping the underprivileged the wrong way."

She twisted to see Rand's face. "He's a hothead who refuses to learn. Tell me, exactly how many years have you wasted trying to teach him about crops and what's needed to maintain the balance for optimal growth?"

He grimaced.

"I rest my case. His burning desire is to be human. I should remove his magic and let him live like the rest of the mortals."

"I recognize that look. Don't do anything you'll regret, Brelenia," he warned. "He's not the only one who's made a muck of things in the past. Those damned sandals of yours—" He groaned when he saw her guilty flush. "What did you do?"

"Nothing!"

"What are you *planning* to do?"

She shrugged a shoulder.

"Woman, if you interfere in his life again, he'll never forgive you."

"Oh, posh! Of course, he will. Besides, didn't you feel the quake?"

He nodded with a dark frown, reminding her of their

wayward son when confronted with something he didn't particularly care for.

"That was Enguerrand kissing his mate."

Rand hung his head. "Wonderful. We're about to have another major catastrophe on our hands."

"Perhaps not," she said slyly, glancing at the box with the magical shoes.

"Brelenia of Messia, don't you dare send those things—"

They disappeared in a puff of smoke, and she grinned her satisfaction. "Too late."

"I need to warn him."

She snapped her fingers, and her clothing fell away.

His surprised blink turned into a hot stare, and his mouth curled into a wide, wicked grin. "What sandals?"

Brelenia laughed and opened her arms.

Tripp Nightshade.

Since their kiss last Wednesday, he'd taken up residence in Elara's mind and refused to leave. The week had led to avoidance on both their parts. By unspoken mutual agreement, they headed in opposite directions whenever they saw each other.

"The least you could do is pay rent, you kissing pirate," she muttered as she cut through the tape of yet another box. When she saw the contents, she groaned. "Flo is going to freaking kill me."

"Why?"

A surprised scream escaped Elara, and she pressed her hand to her throat. "Oh, Pixy Stix, Payton! You know better than to sneak up on me in the storeroom. It's creepier than a graveyard at midnight in here."

Her sister grinned. "You're just a 'fraidy cat, El. Admit it."

"Suck a lemon."

Payton wandered around, picking up random things, blowing

the dust off, and half-heartedly examining them before returning them. "So, why is old Florence going to kill you?"

"I screwed up the order again," Elara admitted. Heat crept up her neck, and she ducked her head to hide her embarrassed flush.

"Again?" Payton frowned and knelt by the box.

Trying to keep her nosy sister from examining its contents, Elara slapped her hands on the cardboard flaps and scowled.

"What are you doing here, anyway? It's not like you read."

With narrowed eyes, Payton peeled Elara's fingers away, one by one, leading to a tussle. Her sister released a triumphant cry when she pinned Elara to the ground and used her for a chair as she dug into the order.

"Vibrators?"

"You don't need to crow about it," she growled, shoving Payton off her. "And why don't you say it louder? I'm sure they didn't hear you across the road at *Wily Witches Brew-Ha-Ha*."

"Oh, pfft. Stop acting like an uptight virgin. Who cares what these people think?"

"Me. And so should you."

"I gave all that up when I dumped Mayor Cobb's son," Payton said, waving her hand in dismissal. Her breezy attitude didn't match the troubled light in her aquamarine eyes. And with good reason! She'd loved Dailey Cobb with her entire being, insisting she'd left him at the altar for his own good.

"Have you seen him since you've been back?"

"At a distance." Her pain was difficult to witness, and Elara hugged her, only to be brushed off. "Our breakup was two years ago, El. It's old news."

"You can kid yourself and the rest of Witchmere, but not me, P. You still care."

"Maybe, but it was for the best. I'm not wifey material," Payton replied, morose.

"Who is?"

They both screeched, nearly falling over when Florence stepped from the shadows.

"What the hell is wrong with you gels? You're powerful witches, and you jump at every shadow."

"In case you didn't know, this attic is horror-story worthy," Elara retorted. "Even Hex refuses to come up here."

"Because that cat is too lazy to move off the sofa. Goddess forbid he'd have to chase a mouse or seek out a meal." A cough rattled in Florence's chest, but it didn't stop her from placing another home-rolled cigarette between her lips.

"Don't you dare light that in here!" Payton jumped up and tossed the offending cigarette away. "Not only are they cancer sticks, but if you drop an ash in this tinderbox, we're likely to be burned alive."

"Bitch, bitch, bitch," Flo muttered. "Besides, fags settle my nerves. Maybe you'd know if you had a puff or two."

"I suspect you roll weed in with that tobacco, so I suppose you've got a point. But skip the toxic crap and go straight to that golden high already."

"You have a hippy heart like your mother, gel."

With a litany of swear words, Payton stormed away.

"Was that necessary, Flo?" Elara asked softly, careful to keep censure from her tone. Her cantankerous old boss hated being in the wrong and turned surly if confronted head-on.

"No. But I see so much of—" The older woman clammed up, compressing her lips as if to lock the words inside.

Elara took a wild guess. "You see so much of my parents? You knew them?"

When they were young, Payton and Elara lived with their parents on the outskirts of this town. But nothing had kept Rupert and Mae Hawthorne in one place for long. As Flo said, they possessed hippy hearts, and their bohemian lifestyle invited scorn.

"Yes," Florence snapped.

Elara stared, waiting her out. Eventually, the old curmudgeon softened, and her gaze dropped to the box.

"Vibrators, hmm?" Florence's laughter surprised Elara. "The first box sold like hot cakes at an all-you-can-eat buffet."

"What?" Aghast, she stared at her boss. "You said you were sending them back!"

"Enguerrand suggested I put them on the social media shopping site. That TickerTape video went vital."

"Viral, and it's Tik—you know what, never mind. Who's Enguerrand? A new beau?"

Florence narrowed her eyes in consideration, then opened her mouth. Whatever she was about to say was lost when Tripp stepped from the shadows.

Elara screamed.

These constant surprises were precisely why she was likely to have a heart attack in this blasted storeroom!

CHAPTER FOUR

Tripp Nightshade.

Here! In her storeroom! Okay, not *hers*, but she worked here, and that sort of made it her space, right?

And he showed up in the middle of an embarrassing conversation! Although it hadn't been thoroughly humiliating until Elara realized he'd been lurking in the shadows and probably heard everything.

With a box full of dildos staring her in the face!

OH, GOD! OH, GOD! OH, GOD!

Don't speak, Elara. Don't speak. Keep your trap shut, or who the hell knows what will come out?

His lips quirked as if he guessed her struggle, and her hard-won cool deserted her. But if she were honest, she'd never *ever* maintained a hard-won cool in her entire life. Hell, she'd never even experienced one, much less maintained it.

Glancing at Florence, Elara had a moment of surprise. Her boss's scowl wasn't standard irritation and appeared as more of a worrisome frown.

What did she have to be concerned about?

Tripp?

In fairness, the power radiating off of him was intense. To a witch of Florence's standing, his presence had to feel like a challenge, especially if she hadn't known he was planning to pop in. Although Tripp frequented *Never Too Many* to pick up his weekly book order, he didn't linger, and Florence rarely spoke to him other than a grudging "Thank you for buying local."

"Uh…" What could Elara say? Ever since the moment he left her in her apartment, in a pool of delirious desire, her ability to speak had been severely hampered. Even on her best day, she wasn't a grand conversationalist, but now? Yeah, well, she was snowed under by all her insecurities.

Seeming to ignore the vibe, he squatted down and fisted a hand in her hair.

"Go away, Flo," he ordered.

He could've knocked Elara over with a heavy sigh when her boss left them alone.

Tilting her head back, Tripp stared moodily at her lips before muttering, "Aww, fuck it."

His mouth covered hers, and it didn't occur to her to object or take offense. Not when she wanted him to kiss her as badly as she did. Like last week, lightning flashed, thunder rumbled, and the earth quaked, but she figured it was her brain exploding inside her skull. Because never in her wildest dreams had she imagined he tasted so wonderful. Or that every delicious swirl of his tongue would bring the decadent flavors of espresso and dark chocolate brownies.

She moaned her pleasure, leaning into him. Before she could register the position shift, she was straddling him and gripping his head hard enough to snap it off his shoulders. The last part was made clear when he reached up and gently tugged her wrists. With a gasp, she rocked backward and stared into his smoldering eyes.

"Is this why every woman throws herself in your path? They've experienced this… this…" She gestured between their faces. "You know. *This*."

His bemused expression transformed to amused, and he grinned.

"Elara, my dear flitter-mouse, what is it you believe I do all day long? Drag unsuspecting townsfolk into dark alleys and kiss them senseless?"

When he put it that way...

She scowled. "No! But I thought maybe a *few*, and people like to brag, so maybe word spread."

"There are rumors about me dragging people into alleyways?"

Narrowing her eyes, she flicked his ear. "You are purposely mocking me."

"Yes, and it's wildly amusing," he admitted, settling his hands on her hips.

"Well, knock it off. I'm not an uptight virgin."

His lips compressed, and she was shocked to see dimples etched in his cheeks. After a two-year-long study of his features, she thought she knew every square inch of his face. How the hell had she missed those delightful dips?

"When did you develop dimples?" she demanded, disregarding both the fact that he was laughing at her *and* he'd labeled her a mouse. He wasn't the only one to ever do either, but his teasing wasn't malicious.

"What?" He didn't bother to hide his humor-filled snort.

"Have you always had them?"

"Always." His gaze grew tender as he stroked the skin along her jawline with his thumb. "Maybe you've simply never seen me with my guard down."

He was right.

"Why? Why is it you're never relaxed enough to laugh or smile?"

"I have. With you," he replied in a patient, wait-for-it tone.

"But..." Thinking back, she recalled that she avoided looking at him whenever she'd believed she'd made a spectacle of herself. Of course, she'd missed seeing him amused! She'd been afraid of his mockery.

Cradling the nape of her neck, he drew her in for a quick buss on the lips. "There it is."

Heat surged into her face.

"Never be embarrassed for being who you are, Elara. You're beautiful."

She froze.

He'd just lied to her.

Baldfaced.

Looking her right in the eye.

Shoving his arms away, she scrambled off him.

"Elara?"

Halfway to the door, she turned back, lifted her chin, and glared. "You're a dick."

"What just happened?" he asked as if he were walking through a wildflower field planted atop landmines.

"You lied!"

Losing his neutral expression, he stared in apparent shock. *"What?"*

"I'm plain, not beautiful. And you can take your stupid games elsewhere, Tripp Nightshade! I won't be made fun of."

She ran.

"Escape! Escape! Escape!" drummed through her mind, drowning out everything but her panicked need to flee.

Left sitting next to a box of super-sized dildos, Tripp was stupefied.

"Well, don't *you* feel like an asshole?" a female asked him.

He glanced up in time to see Elara's sister lean away from the wall she'd been resting against. With one leg propped up and the other swinging back and forth alongside the trunk she perched upon, she blew a giant pink bubble. When it popped, she peeled it off her face, shoved it in her mouth, and masticated the gum.

"Yes, and I don't understand why," he agreed with a head shake. Drawing his legs up to hide his semi-erection from making out with Elara, he looped his arms, clasping his hands together. "Got any clues as to why your sister doesn't believe she's worthy of praise?"

"Plenty. None I'm willing to share with you." Payton rose and sauntered around the room.

"How long have you been sitting there? Cloaked, if I'm not mistaken."

And how the hell had she managed to avoid detection? Surely he wasn't so distracted by Elara to leave himself vulnerable? Recalling their kiss and her swollen, glistening lips, he had to allow he might've been.

"Not long," Payton admitted. "About the time she said she wasn't an uptight virgin."

She cast a significant glance at the box and smirked. The look was telling.

"Your sister's a virgin?" He wanted to slam his head against the wall as penance for being stupid.

Payton rolled her eyes. "Dude. Is *any* female a virgin over eighteen?"

"Don't make it sound like she's promiscuous," he growled, irritated on Elara's behalf. "She's not."

"Sorry." Contrition was reflected on her lovely face. "I didn't mean it that way. It's just, I don't know any person who hasn't had a sexual encounter. Elara included."

He nodded but found his irritation had increased instead of dying away. The idea of Elara with anyone but him was triggering.

"Right. Well, I'll leave you to… uh, all this…" Tripp stood, barely catching himself from gesturing to the adult toys. The action would go over like a lead balloon, especially when he only meant for her to tag and ship them.

Her expression turned uncomfortable, and she opened her mouth twice before closing it again.

"What is it, Payton?"

"Could you, um, not let anyone know you've seen me?"

"Dailey doesn't know you're back?" he asked.

"No, and I'd like to keep it that way." Her chin pointed skyward, and in her defiant gesture, he saw the resemblance to Elara. The look, more than anything, had him agreeing.

As he turned to go, he remembered what he'd come for. Tripp scanned the rickety old shelves until his gaze touched on the package calling to him.

Those blasted boots!

They equaled catastrophe.

Reaching for them, he received the shock of his life.

Literal electrocution.

And the zap sent him flying backward, straight into Elara's box of dildos.

They scattered, and everywhere one looked, there was a plethora of pleasure sticks.

Payton stared in horrified amusement. With her palms pressed to her mouth, she did her damnedest not to laugh.

"Did you do that?" he growled.

"What?"

"Charm that package."

Her gaze followed his to the bane of his existence, and she shook her head, eyes wide with wonder.

With a savage curse, he rose and approached the box addressed to Elara, then swore again. Twice as long and three times as loud.

His hiding spot was blown, and it meant disappearing.

Pronto.

But he couldn't leave this mess at Elara's door. Mother had not only found *him*, she had found the one woman who would destroy an entire town if he left her with the fatal footwear. It wasn't the first time Brelenia of Messia had sent them to a female she believed Tripp was interested in, but this time, he intended to see they were weighted in cement and dropped at the bottom of the ocean. Elara wasn't equipped to deal with the fallout if he didn't.

He was gearing up to attempt another snatch and run when

the bloody thing vanished with a poof of smoke. The sinking-in-quicksand sensation he experienced stole his breath, and he feared hyperventilating.

"What was in the box?" Payton had enough presence of mind to be wary of him and the item he'd fixated on.

"Something that I should've destroyed a long time ago."

"Why was it addressed to my sister?"

He met her worried gaze. Payton was right to be fearful, and he appreciated the hell out of her instincts. "We need to get to your sister before she opens it. Come on!"

CHAPTER FIVE

Tripp Nightshade.

He'd kissed her again!

Then, Elara had drummed up the nerve to call him a liar. Where her gumption came from was anyone's guess, but she was proud of herself.

"You should've seen me, Hex," she told her cat as she gathered her mail. "I was a badass!"

As they traversed the hallway to her apartment, she explained how she'd given Tripp what-for. Once they were safely ensconced in the living room, Hex hiked a leg and did what he always did when Tripp's name was mentioned—he licked his balls.

"Rude," she muttered. "One day, I'm going to remember to get a spray bottle to cure you of your bad habit."

Hex paused to give his best I-will-fuck-you-up-and-shit-on-everything-you-own look.

"Oh, pearlescent Pixy Stix, Hex. You know I'll never spray you with water. I'd be taking my life into my hands."

Satisfied she'd been duly warned, he returned to his business, and Elara would swear he was more aggressive in his actions.

Ignoring him, she untied the hemp twine securing the package. No return address or other identifying marks indicated where it had originated. This close to Christmas, anyone could expect to receive a gift or two, but Payton was the only one Elara was close to, and it was doubtful she stopped to consider anyone else long enough to send a present. Many years ago, Elara realized that the only person who would treat her to anything was herself.

The surprise came when she lifted the lid.

Her gasp caused Hex to pause his ministrations and shift for a better view.

"Meow?" There was a definite question in the sound.

"I don't know who sent them. But these boots are gorgeous!"

And they were.

Made of deep amethyst-dyed leather, they were ankle-high and had a three-inch heel. What appeared to be genuine quartz was cut to display the gemstone to advantage and decorated the vamp. Smaller rhinestones, as shiny and clear as any diamonds she'd seen, were arranged in an intricate pattern around the amethyst jewels. Of varying sizes, they wound over the arch and up along the quarter next to a row of eyelets. The laces were made of chenille, and dangling from the ends were more gemstones of varying shapes and sizes.

And they were perfect!

If Elara were a shoe designer, these bad boys would put her on the map to fame and fortune. Only the rich and famous could afford them, for damned sure. But who had sent them to her? Certainly not Tripp. How would he know she was a size six and a half?

When she picked one up, she felt a zing. If asked, she couldn't say if that was because of the joyful feeling they gave her or the sheer beauty of the boot. Walking to her window, she held it up and marveled at how the sun's rays caught the facets of the stones, creating a light show inside the room.

"I love them," she whispered.

The feeling of being watched washed over her, and she glanced downward at the street.

Tripp and Payton had stopped on the sidewalk and stared at her. Her sister with concern, and him with horror.

Firm resolve stiffened her spine.

"Just once, I wish you'd see me as something more than a joke, Tripp Nightshade," she said with conviction. "See that I can be wicked and worthy of your lofty self. Oh, what I wouldn't give to make you kneel at my feet and profess your undying love!"

The shoe in her hand heated up, and one by one, the jewels lit, pulsing with a breathtaking green glow.

"Very *Close Encounters*," she murmured, fascinated by the display, disappointed she didn't hear the movie's orchestral theme in time to the repeated rhythm of flashing lights.

Footsteps thundered up the stairs, and the banging on her door was obnoxiously loud. Compelled to ignore it, she kicked off her sneakers, straightened her sock, and drew on the first boot. It felt like Heaven in a shoe, and she hopped from one foot to the other, standing taller with each press of her heel. Satisfied with the fit, she drew on the other and sighed.

Perfect!

Tingling started in her lower extremities and traveled upward. She pressed her thighs together as the wave of heat started a fire in her lady cave, similar to the feeling Tripp had created with his kisses. The next surge of warmth caused her stomach to tighten, and her breasts became heavy as her nipples contracted into tight buds. She never wanted to have sex more than in that moment, and if Tripp happened to walk through her door, he wouldn't know what hit him.

"Elara! Open the door!"

Why didn't he use his power like the last time? She'd have welcomed the magical muscle display.

"*Elara!*"

The ground rumbled, like when they'd kissed. His desperate voice coursed through her, and she closed her eyes at the thrilling tickle it created. A purr escaped her throat. She wanted him to stroke her all over. Pet her like a cat. Lick her pus—

The door slammed back on its hinges, and there he was, resembling an enraged bull. Breathing hard, eyes wild, face flushed.

He was magnificent!

Tripp's gaze widened as it swept over her hot face and down her body, and he looked decidedly ill at ease the second he noticed her new boots.

"Take those off." His voice was just above a croak. "Do it, Elara. Do it now."

Feeling wicked, powerful, and decidedly rebellious, she laughed. The husky voice wasn't her own. Or it had never been in the past. New Elara appreciated it, though.

"If you want to have sex with me, Tripp, you need only ask." She winked, then giggled as his jaw dropped. Smoothing her hands down her breasts, over her abdomen, and finally, along the curve of her hips, she grinned. "Or maybe not. Maybe I require a man willing to *take* what he wants."

An outraged flush began at his neck, riding the skin along his clenched jaw to settle on his high cheekbones.

Oh, those incredible cheekbones!

Third only to those penetrating dark eyes that were second to his glorious, glorious shoulders.

"How about you remove your shirt first?" she suggested, sashaying to him.

He seemed frozen to the spot, incapable of complying. Once she reached him, she pressed her hand over his pounding heart.

Stretching up, she ran her nose the length of his chiseled jawline, inhaling his intoxicating scent. "Why, Tripp Nightshade! If I didn't know better, I'd say you were in awe of little ol' me."

"Elara?" Payton's voice caused a strange effect, like lightning crackling through Elara's veins. "Hey, sis."

A wave of dizziness caused her to sway, sending her stumbling sideways. Tripp caught her in a stunningly quick move that stole what was left of her breath. The muscled arm supporting her waist was pure steel and caused her blood to hum.

"Yes," she whispered, meeting his burning gaze. "The answer will always be yes."

"No," he ground out. "Mine will always be *no*."

Instantaneous fury, born from his rejection and her humiliation, exploded in her brain.

How dare he?

Twice, he'd kissed her as if she were his everything. And now he treated her like she was beneath him? Like her invitation disgusted him?

"Screw you," she snapped.

Not expecting to budge him, Elara shoved. She gasped in shock when his arm fell away, and he stumbled back into the wall. A two-foot-tall, watercolor hummingbird print crashed to the floor, and Hex hissed his displeasure before bolting into the bedroom.

"What the hell is happening?" Payton cried.

Another wave of irritation crashed over Elara.

"None of your damned business," she snarled. "Now get the hell out."

Tripp's arm shot out, and he gripped Payton's wrist. "Don't. Don't go. I'm going to need you for what's next."

"What do you mean? My magic?" Her look said he was fifty cards shy of a full deck. "It's basic, and if you think I'd do anything to hurt my sister, you've lost your entire bag of marbles, buddy!"

Elara smirked, happy her sister had her back. She experienced a moment's pause but didn't stop to examine why her emotions were ping-ponging all over the place.

"Get out, Tripp." She flung her hand toward the door. "Payton can stay."

"Sorry, flitter-mouse, but I'm not going anywhere," he said regretfully. "I need those boots."

"You can fuck all the way off," she said with faux sweetness. "They were a gift, and I'm keeping them."

"Elara—"

Concentrating all her energy on giving him a different kind of boot, she clapped.

Tripp climbed from the frozen lake, too burning mad to feel the icy wind against his soaked body.

The ground rumbled in answer to his rage. Inhaling deeply, he expelled a breath to the count of ten. Closing his eyes, he concentrated on warming his body, starting with the nucleus of his cells and working outward to his organs and extremities. When he was done, his clothes were dry and warm again. Thank the Gods! If he'd been mortal, he'd be dead from the hypothermia caused by Elara's little stunt.

Those fucking boots!

"What the hell were you thinking, Mother?" he muttered aloud.

"Oh, I don't know. Perhaps you'd do the proper thing for once?" Brelenia answered.

He half spun and spotted her about ten feet away, as pretty as you please, on a blanket behind an enormous picnic basket.

"Come, Enguerrand. I've had Eloisa prepare us a lovely meal."

"I should murder you and be done with it," he said conversationally as he approached her. "What makes you believe I would break bread with you after this latest stunt?"

Her warm smile drew him in, as it always had. His mother was a master manipulator.

"I wish you to find a mate and be happy, darling boy. Running from your fate is useless."

"Oh, I don't know." Tripp sprawled on his side and took the proffered bunch of grapes. "I've managed it most of my life and am perfectly content."

"Content. Not happy."

He paused with a grape halfway to his mouth.

She was right, damn her!

"You're growing up," she observed. "There was a time when your denial would've been immediate. At least now, you've stopped to think about what I've said."

Rarely would he ask her for anything, but the idea of a magical object changing Elara into a spiteful, wicked woman hurt his heart. "Please, Mother. Take the boots back and be done with this latest game."

Brelenia cocked her head and studied him for a long moment before pouring him a glass of wine.

"Is that a no?" he asked softly, taking a sip and savoring the flavor of the rich, red beverage.

"It's a no." She held up a hand when he would've argued for her to do the proper thing. "Not because I don't want to, darling. But they're charmed, and you must see their latest mischief through to the end."

"What will it take to avert disaster?"

"Why do you believe they'll bring disaster?"

"Oh, I don't know." Sitting up, he tossed the wine onto the grass and dropped the glass into the basket. The waste of a good vino would piss her off, and Tripp wasn't above being petty in the face of her manipulation. "Perhaps the countless calamities of the past. The Great London Fire in 1666. The French Revolution and Napoleon's rise."

"That was on you, darling. You fell for that peasant girl and fed into the uprising."

"Yeah, well, you didn't have to give her those blasted boots!" he retorted.

"I'll admit it wasn't well done of me. Who knew she was connected with that upstart Napoleon? He was the gift that kept giving, wasn't he?" Brelenia waved a hand in dismissal. "But the past is the past, Enguerrand."

"That's the point, Mother." He scrubbed his face with his hands and expelled a heavy breath. "As if the Great London Fire wasn't enough, we had to repeat that little event with the Great Chicago Fire."

"I truly believed *that* silly twit was more clever than I gave her credit for," she protested. "Really, darling, you need to be more selective."

Tripp threw up his hands. "Stop with this madness. I'm begging you. You can't keep playing with people's lives." He pressed his thumb to his right eye socket. "I swear to Zeus, I develop an eye twitch every time those damned things appear. They're a harbinger of doom, and poor Elara is the biggest disaster in town."

"That's not nice to say about your beloved," Brelenia reprimanded.

"She's *not* my beloved!"

"Oh." Mother tapped her teeth with a fingernail. "That might be part of the problem."

"Why?"

"The shoes or, in Elara's case, boots should only be worn by the person you love. They are meant to grant the wearer's fondest wish. If she desires you, but you don't care about her in return, she'll go mad." She shot him a side glance. "Clearly, that's what happened all those past times. I mean, take Petunia. That woman wasn't in her right mind—"

"Drop it," he barked. "How do we clean up your current mess?"

"*My* current mess?" She laughed and began packing the basket. "Oh, no, dear boy. It's your problem now."

"Mother, *please*."

She smiled when she patted his cheek like she had when he was a small boy. "Perhaps settle down with this one. When she's happy, those boots will move on. After all, they're made for witching."

With a dark frown, Tripp looked at the half-frozen lake.

"Why were you swimming on such a blustery day, darling? And fully clothed?"

He sent her a sharp glance, searching for the underlying guile. If one looked closely, they'd see it in her twinkling burnt-amber eyes.

"As if you don't already know," he said in disgust.

"She has more power than she realizes if she can toss you across town." Brelenia rose and smoothed her white gown down her legs. "Whose child is she?"

"She had hippies for parents," he said, hoping to hide what little he knew of Elara's origins. No need to feed his mother's obsession with the knowledge of a perfect match. If Brelenia of Messia discovered Elara Hawthorne's true heritage, she'd become even more relentless.

"Hippies? I'm not familiar with the term."

Pressing her lips together in thought caused her dimples to appear, which then reminded Tripp of Elara's question. Odd how they never appeared until either he or Mother was amused.

"No need to worry about the term or what's happening here. But I want your promise; this is the last time," he said.

"Oh, I suspect it will *definitely* be the last time."

CHAPTER SIX

It only occurred to him *after* his mother vanished that she hadn't promised a fucking thing. She'd taken the food and plaid blanket, leaving the lingering scent of springtime in her wake.

Tripp inhaled deeply, savoring the smell of orange blossoms after a rain. His mother's unique fragrance always returned him to childhood and brought a sense of calm despite the havoc she created. However, neither the scent nor the peace lasted as he considered the problem of Elara and the boots.

He approached the shoreline and stared at the gray horizon, considering the problem. No matter how he examined it, whatever the angle, he knew Elara was fucked, right along with Witchmere—and not with those blasted dildos! Perhaps it was time to call his father and ask what he'd done when Brelenia wore them during their tumultuous courtship. Surely he'd have some sage advice to offer, right?

An explosion rocked the air, causing Tripp to stumble. His leather loafers skidded on the icy embankment, and down he plunged, swearing viciously. The energy behind his vehement response released a shockwave, and the local wildlife ran for their lives.

He scrambled out of the water and recalled his power to him. The spontaneous surge wouldn't have happened if his emotions hadn't been dangerously close to the surface. It would be best to keep his feelings buried for the foreseeable future to avoid chaos at every turn.

Archer Roche, the last of a dying breed of blacksmiths, appeared at the edge of the woods, a frown tugging his bushy ginger-colored brows together. He was a mountain of a man, and to look at him, one wouldn't immediately recognize the power he hid.

But Tripp knew.

He possessed an extensive dossier on every citizen in Witchmere. Of necessity, he'd collected facts and made a point of slyly interviewing the townsfolk to see if their abilities were a threat to him. Some he befriended, others he kept at a respectful distance.

Like Archer.

Gargoyles were notorious loners, taking their job to protect a village seriously, thereby distrusting newcomers like Tripp. Over the years, as wars and raiding became less frequent, their kind died off, until only a handful remained. Most of those still alive resided in out-of-the-way places.

Archer Roche was the oldest and most formidable. But his time would eventually come, too.

Soon, if Tripp couldn't control the narrative with those fucking enchanted boots.

Sighing, he trudged up the hill, drying and warming himself as he went. By the time he'd reached Archer, he was once again his standard pristine self. Yes, he preferred jeans and a soft sweater over heavy clothing, but he also preferred to be *clean*. He was obsessive about it. That's why two dunks in that algae-filled lake had made his skin crawl, and his need for a shower was pressing.

Or maybe his unease stemmed from what was to come.

He glanced toward the origin of the explosion. "What the hell *was* that, Roche?"

"You said you wanted to know if anything ever happened to Elara Haw—"

Not waiting for the rest, Tripp teleported.

When he arrived at her apartment building and saw it intact, he surveyed the town.

Dailey Cobb's police cruiser flew past, with blue lights circling and sirens drowning out any other noise. After waiting and watching to see which direction the officer was headed, Tripp closed his eyes and concentrated on Elara's energy. Satisfied she was unhurt and close, he visualized the alley beside the bookstore.

The skin-scorching heat from the raging inferno was the first thing he felt as he materialized. A discordant symphony of emergency vehicle horns and sirens was the next to register. At the end of the alley, Florence and Payton huddled, with Elara pacing a hole in the asphalt beside them.

"What the hell happened, Sanderson?" he asked Bohdan, sensing the shifter in the shadows.

"Don't know. But regular magic couldn't extinguish the flames, so they called the fire department."

Across the distance, Tripp met Elara's furious gaze, and with a certainty he felt to his bones, he knew she was fueling it. Likely without even being aware. That problem needed to be rectified.

Quickly.

Pasting on a soft smile, he approached her. His attention appeared to startle her, and her rage subsided a small degree, causing the heat from the blaze to lessen.

"Someone blew up Flo's place!" she said, anger simmering in her large eyes.

Tripp noted two things. First, she'd lost her standard shyness around him. Second, she acted as if she expected him to produce a suspect on the spot so she could pulverize them. The prior, he could appreciate, though he mourned the loss of her rosy blushes. The latter, well, odds were the culprit was none other than herself, though she wouldn't recognize those bloody boots were the problem.

Tripp cupped her cheek as she turned her face to him, and he brushed a thumb along her jawline. "Don't worry, flitter-mouse. The person responsible will be caught."

Hell, he'd already caught her, but the reveal required finesse and those leather menaces to be off her feet. Maybe he could seduce her out of them *without* it culminating in a sexual act. In no way was he adding sex to the mix until she had bare feet.

His dick twitched, already taking the news badly.

He could hear it now...

Good luck with that, buddy! You have no restraint around her.

Ignoring his internal dialogue, he focused on the situation at hand.

"I'm going to put the fire out, Elara," he said, pitching his voice toward seduction. "Will you give me a kiss for luck?"

With her desires heightened by the enchantment, she didn't even question him or his motives, and her gaze zeroed in on his mouth. Nodding, she licked her lips. Sure, he should've felt bad for conning her, but one did whatever it took in the pursuit of saving a townful of people, right?

Dipping his head, he captured the eager mouth she offered.

Although he'd been prepared for the elemental display, the lightning strike still startled him, as did the ground rumble. Their proximity to Mount Rainier was nerve-wracking. It would take nothing to wake that great beast if their earthshaking exchanges continued in this vein. Yet her curvy body pressed against his shorted out the hardwiring of his brain. His need to get closer, to feel her fully against him, overrode his common sense and the urgency to put out the fire.

Someone with balls of steel dumped an icy drink down Tripp's neck, and he turned with a snarl.

Florence, solemn but unrepentant, nodded toward the fire. "If you please."

"Fuck." He ran a shaking hand through his hair, absently noticing the local rubberneckers watching him with expressions akin to shock. Public displays of affection weren't his usual M.O.

He avoided showing anyone favor. Kissing Elara, in what equated to a town gathering, was garnering attention he'd rather not have.

"Wait here," he said to Flo and the Hawthorne sisters.

Striding past the firefighters and emergency responders, Tripp entered the inferno. The hair on the back of his neck rose as he sensed another presence behind him.

A powerful one.

The sound of stone scraping against stone told him who was present and that Archer had shifted into his gargoyle form. Likely, he was there to protect Tripp from falling beams. The man had earned himself a demigod's undying appreciation and a case of expensive whisky.

Moving to the center of the room, Tripp raised his arms and tilted his palms upward, centering himself. Next, he considered the elements he was dealing with: fire and air. Good thing the rock man didn't need to breathe, and that Tripp was able to hold his breath as long as necessary, because the next step was to suck all the oxygen from the room with one consuming inhale.

Denied its fuel, the blazing elemental turned angry and licked at his legs. Its goal was to claim a victim. Anyone would do.

Simple visualization pushed the flames back from him and Archer. Concentrating on the heat, Tripp folded it in on itself like a paper napkin, making it smaller and smaller until only a tiny section remained. One box held the blaze in check, but the trade-off was the toxic fumes released by melting dildos. Surprised at seeing Elara's accidental purchase, he almost lost control of the fire.

Standing over the box, arms extended—similar to a person warming their hands at a bonfire—he shook his head. Any doubt he might've had about this mishap being the result of those fucking boots was gone. The truth was, if the witch wearing them weren't skilled, like Elara, disasters would happen.

They were, after all, designed by a Trickster.

Mother had said they granted wishes, but Tricksters, like

Djinn, always exacted a price for providing that which wasn't fated or freely given.

Angry on behalf of Elara, who was the innocent in his mother's schemes, Tripp used more force than necessary to subdue the flames. Deformed pleasure plungers flew in every direction, slamming into and sticking against walls, cabinets, burnt books, and, worst of all, Archer Roche. Other than a narrow-eyed glare, the human boulder remained mute.

As the gargoyle shifted to leave, one of a dozen hot-pink vibrators plastered to the ceiling dropped and stuck on what constituted Archer's ass, creating a colorful, misshapen tail.

Tripp's horrified bark of laughter rang out and unleashed a minor shockwave.

"Run!" he shouted, bolting for the exit.

Melting vibrators and charred paperbacks pelted them as they ran the gauntlet of the romance book aisle. Believing he was home free, he slowed at the door to look back. A foot-long dong smacked him right between the eyes, eliciting a curse. He should've remembered Lot's wife.

And fuck all, because if that wasn't a portent of the dreadful things to come, Tripp didn't know what was.

CHAPTER SEVEN

Tripp Nightshade.

Elara didn't know what the hell to think. One second, he rejects her, and the next, he kisses her like a soldier returning home from war, ignoring an entire town of onlookers.

She worried her fingernails between her teeth until he exited the building. The mammoth ginger-haired man next to him bent double, laughing, as Tripp scowled and rubbed a penis-shaped mark in the center of his forehead.

His stormy gaze locked with hers across the distance, and an anticipatory thrill ran the entire length of her body, causing her nipples to tighten in response. Those wonderfully long legs of his ate up the distance between them, and he never lost focus as people tried to speak to him or praise him for his heroic deeds.

When he arrived before her, he held out a hand, which she dutifully clasped. His stride was brisk, and she was forced to trot to keep up.

"Tripp! Slow down! I can't run in these things."

He stopped short and gave her boots a considering look. "Then take them off."

"There's snow on the ground, in case you hadn't noticed." She scoffed and shook her head. "So, no. Not a chance."

"Take them off and hop on my back. I'll carry them to your place." A roguish grin bolstered his gallant offer, but something about his expression was wrong, and it took a moment to realize what.

"The dimples are missing," she murmured.

His brows rose in question. "What?"

"Your dimples are missing, meaning you're being fake. *Again*."

Appearing to fight a jaw drop, he won, but only just. Rounding on her, he crossed his arms over his chest, accidentally or purposely drawing her eyes to those magnificently sculpted pectoral muscles outlined beneath his black sweater. Forgetting anything but the sheer perfection of his body, she let her gaze linger on those delicious shoulders she wanted so desperately to nibble.

He snapped his fingers.

"My eyes are up here," he said dryly.

"Yes, but I'm ogling your shoulders. I'm in lust with them," she admitted. Once she'd realized what she said, horror sent blood rushing to her face, and her desire to escape was profound. But a sudden calm pervaded, halting her embarrassment.

Were her feet tingling? *Odd*.

"Oh, Elara Elizabeth Hawthorne, you are clueless. There you are, toying with the lid of Pandora's box."

His use of her full name did what nothing else could've and caught her wayward attention.

"How do you know my middle name?"

Was it weird that he did? What the hell did it mean?

A muscle worked in his jaw as if he were undecided or angry. Call it instinct, but she doubted it was the latter.

"Tripp? How do you know my middle name?"

"I may have googled you when we first met," he admitted. His reddening neck spread into a flushed visage, and she detected a hint of chagrin on his face. But he didn't meet her gaze, and the avoidance was telling.

"But I'm not special, am I?" she concluded. "I'm not the only one whose information you gathered. Who else? My sister? Other women?"

His color deepened.

"Ohmygawd! You're a pervert!"

"I'm *not* a pervert!" he shouted.

Nearby, startled birds took to the skies, and tiny, city-dwelling creatures stopped foraging for winter food to seek safety. But Elara wasn't scared of him. Quite the opposite. The idea of an imperfect Tripp Nightshade was positively delightful.

Lifting a brow, she smirked. "You are!"

"Elara, I swear to Zeus—"

Thunder rumbled, long and loud, causing him to glance skyward.

She would've sworn she heard him mutter, "Sorry, Uncle." But of a certainty, he couldn't be related to the king of Gods, right? Her eyes, naughty and possessing a mind of their own, leisurely traveled the length of his body before making a slower return trip north.

Or perhaps he *was*.

Envisioning his body chiseled in marble and displayed at some museum was easy.

A random thought popped into her head. "How old *are* you?"

"Pardon?" His black brows shot to his hairline so fast she was surprised they didn't launch themselves off his forehead.

"Sometimes your speech and mannerisms tell on you. We all know witches don't age like mortals. The more magic a person has, the slower their aging process." She shrugged. "The few times we kissed, I tasted the suppressed power."

He remained silent, confirming her suspicions.

Taking a step forward, she traced a heart on his chest. "That old, huh?"

His sudden chuckle rumbled, causing Elara's fingers to vibrate wherever they made contact. A warming sensation shot through her, landing squarely in her FuFu Land. The flood of heat to her vagina made her uncomfortably wet.

A first, for sure!

Lovers in the past had left her disappointed, but instinct told her Tripp wasn't like them. If he set out to do something like give her a Holiday Hallelujah, he wouldn't quit until she was screeching "Gloria" in a high-soprano C-note at over a thousand hertz.

"Earth to Elara," he teased, recalling her from adding things to her naughty-would-definitely-be-nice list. Wouldn't Santa be shocked?

"Right, so you're ancient, and you like younger women. Got it."

He laughed. "I'm not ancient, not for what I am."

"Which is?" she prompted, drawing out the "zzz" sound.

"Nothing you need to concern yourself with, little girl," he growled. The sparkling humor in his eyes belied his fierceness, and she laughed.

Why was she freer with him, in this moment, than she had ever been in her entire life? Never before had she felt seen, much less interesting. How could she, dumpy and shy Elara Elizabeth Hawthorne, hold his attention for longer than two minutes? Was it the wish she'd made? Was he only attracted to her because of the boots he claims are magical? Or was he using her to get them for himself? Maybe he intended them for another.

"Your aura darkened," he said in a gentle voice. "What's wrong, flitter-mouse?"

Avoidance was her go-to; she always played that card when things turned too introspective. At least outside of her therapist's office, she did.

"I'm fine," she said with a breezy smile. "I'm just wondering if I'll have a job tomorrow."

She'd bet money she didn't have his sharp-eyed perusal saw through her, but he was too polite to call her on her bull chips, which was another indication of his age. No one under the age of forty would let it go. They'd badger her until she lost her shit or confessed to everything from lusting after Tripp Nightshade to steaming open Christmas presents, beginning at age seven. The steaming, not the lusting. That she hadn't done until she'd first seen him two and a half years ago. Although it could be argued he'd made her hot enough to put off steam.

"You'll have a job," he assured her. "Florence isn't going to dismiss you for setting fire to the dildos."

She was preparing a pithy response to his first comment when the second sunk in. "I didn't set them on fire! I wasn't anywhere close to the bookstore. Why would you blame me?"

Tripp narrowed his eyes and considered Elara's question. If she hadn't set the box on fire, then who? The Trickster's signature had been there, and he'd swear it resulted from those blasted boots. Hadn't he experienced more than one epic fire in his lifetime? If not the fraught-with-danger footwear, then what?

"My mistake," he countered smoothly. "I believed Florence would've had you inventorying and pricing them for sale."

The distaste on Elara's face was priceless, and he couldn't resist commenting.

"You don't like dildos?" he asked with every ounce of innocence he could muster.

Scarlet-faced, she glared. "I'm sure it's no business of yours, Tripp Nightshade."

"I beg to differ." Her jaw sagged, and he gave in to the urge to tap her mouth closed. "You've been undressing me with your gorgeous eyes for quite some time now, Elara Hawthorne. You've even gone so far as to proposition me earlier today. That's to say nothing of the kisses we've shared. Seems to me, I should know the preferences of a future lover."

She sucked in a breath so fast she choked, and Tripp lightly thumped her back, taking wicked delight in her coughing fit.

Elara knocked his hand away with a growl. "I'm getting coal for Christmas."

His brows snapped together as his annoyance spiked. "Who's Cole?"

"Coal. C-o-a-l, not C-o-l-e."

Feeling like a colossal idiot for his spontaneous jealousy, Tripp shrugged.

As she stomped away, he remained where he was, appreciating the angry swish of her hips.

"You forgot to get the boots."

He yelped his surprise and spun, searching for Payton Hawthorne. Only, she wasn't easily visible. With a furtive glance around, Tripp stepped into the alley between *Wily Witches Brew-Ha-Ha* and *The Cook's Cauldron*, both popular spots for Elara. By extension, they had become his, though he'd never admit to stalking. If they happened to be in the exact location at the same time, it looked coincidental, right? And if her flustered appearance gave him a small thrill, it was a secret he'd take to the grave.

"They're difficult to remember when I'm with her," he told Payton.

"I'll say. Maybe if you could keep your mind on the objective and not on seducing my sister, you'd be able to get them back."

He didn't dare inform her that if seducing Elara was necessary to get those fucking boots, he'd do it without a second thought—or even a first. Deep down existed the knowledge that if he did, he'd be forever fucked. And not in a good way. The guilt would probably eat him alive, yet the memory of holding her would live with him for eternity.

"What about you?" he asked Payton. "Can you play up the sisterhood card and see if she'll let you try them on?"

"It might work if we were the same shoe size. She's a six and a half. I'm a nine."

"Okay, we'll need to get them while she's sleeping," he said with a definitive nod.

"I'm not sure I want to take part in this. You still haven't convinced me they're anything more than a confidence booster."

Payton was about to say something else, but clammed up the second Dailey Cobb stepped into view. Their eyes connected across the distance, and storm clouds gathered on the officer's ruggedly handsome face. Payton, on the other hand, looked like she'd eaten live eels and was about to regurgitate them back up.

"What's going on here?" Dailey demanded. "When did you return to town?"

Finding her backbone, she squared her shoulders, exactly like Tripp had seen Elara do a hundred times. Two abandoned sisters against the world.

"None of your business, Dailey Cobb," she replied stiffly. "You can go back to enforcing your mommy's rules."

The Hawthorne women were fond of using the NOYB phrase, and it seemed it didn't sit any better with Dailey than it had with Tripp.

"Everything is fine, Officer Cobb," Tripp said with a friendly smile. "Payton and I were discussing the incident at *Never Too Many*. It's shocking, isn't it?"

Dailey's gaze never moved from Payton, but he addressed Tripp. "I can't say it is if the Hawthornes are around."

"Oh, so you're pulling the 'girl from the wrong side of the tracks' routine?" She scoffed, fisting her hands on her hips. "Good one."

One had to listen closely to hear the hurt in her voice, but it existed. Hers was the attitude of a rebel, but underneath her sassy exterior beat the heart of a wounded girl.

Dailey had the grace to blush. "I didn't mean it that way, Payton. You know I didn't."

"Then you're implying my sister and I are bad luck?" she asked an octave higher with rage brewing in her aquamarine eyes.

"Officer Cobb, I'm sure you have better things to do now that you've ascertained everything is fine here. If it worries you that we're in the alley, we'll gladly move to the main street," Tripp said, hoping to defuse the explosive atmosphere.

"Nah." Dailey's drawl was dismissive. "I don't give a damn one way or another, other than to keep this town safe from *trouble*. Have a nice evening, Nightshade."

"You don't give a damn about my sister?" Elara asked from the mouth of the alley. "What the hell kind of thing is *that* to say, Dailey Cobb?"

Her anger brought with it a thick line of dark thunderclouds. Everyone but her glanced up at the first rumblings.

"You were *engaged*, and she loves you," she continued, oblivious to the brewing storm.

"Elara! Please leave it alone." Payton was frantic, and Dailey watched her through narrowed eyes.

"No. He can't treat you like that. None of them can!" Elara stalked to her sister's side and gripped her hand. "Aren't you sick of it? I know I am. What do you want, sissy?" she asked softly.

"To take away the love he feels," Payton said in a low voice. "I don't want him to hurt anymore."

The heavy scent of cloves filled the air, and on the current, Tripp detected a faint purple light. Before he could put a stop to the spell, it encircled Dailey. His expression blanked, and his eyes turned from their brilliant silver to a dull cement color. For a heart-stopping moment, the officer's face grayed, and Tripp thought maybe Elara had accidentally stolen the man's life force. But with a deep, gasping breath, Dailey's color returned to the sunkissed tan it was prior.

"Go away, Dailey," Elara ordered. "Leave my sister alone."

Still dazed, he tipped an imaginary hat in her direction, then wordlessly strode away.

The incident assured Tripp that Elara had a fundamental understanding of what her new magical footwear could do. Retrieving them, however, just got a whole lot trickier.

"*Fuck.*" He wanted to bang his head against the wall. His

mother had a lot to answer for, and although not Tripp's primary problem, he had to remove the curse Elara had activated on Dailey.

CHAPTER EIGHT

Tripp Nightshade.

What was he doing hiding in an alley with Payton yesterday? Whatever it was, he'd triggered Dailey's green-eyed monster. Elara hadn't gone far before she'd gotten the courage to turn back to tell Tripp where he could shove those damned dildos. The second she spun around, she saw him and Payton duck between the buildings like shady co-conspirators. From her vantage point, Elara could see it also sent a red flag up Dailey's pole. He'd missed her approach, but she'd overheard everything, including the pain in Payton's voice.

And that wouldn't do!

With a wave of outrage came a feeling of empowerment, and she'd confronted him on his lie. Anyone with eyes in their head could see his tortured expression and how his attention never wavered from Payton. He was a man obsessed, and hurting, like her sister. Yet he would never understand that his overbearing attitude was the problem, in addition to his mother.

Mayor Mary-Alice Cobb was a royal bitch. As a member of Witchmere's oldest family, she believed her ca-ca didn't stink, but in her arrogance, she dealt out the worst-smelling crap imaginable. And she'd heaped it by the ton on Payton, who wasn't good enough for her precious boy. Dailey had never been able to see it, which made matters worse and Payton miserable.

He had viewed his holier-than-thou directives as helping Payton rein in her inner wild child, but he'd controlled her to the point of rebellion, where escape had become a driving need. She'd fled their wedding and Witchmere, leaving Elara alone with no one for two years.

Elara hadn't expected him to listen to her when she ordered him away. Nor had she expected Tripp's vehement reaction afterward.

"You've got to stop using magic," he'd warned. "You can't even *think* in terms of wishes or the like."

"What are you talking about?" Her unease had grown to a sickening degree, causing her stomach to churn. "I didn't use magic. I—"

"You *did*. Trickster magic, and trust me, it won't be without consequence. We must figure out a way to undo it, and fast, or there could be lasting effects."

His condemnation stung, and she'd have wished him to the North Pole if he hadn't cautioned her against it. With a glare at her boots, he'd left her alone with a very shaken Payton.

And her sister now refused to speak to her.

What had she done so wrong? Stand up against a bully? Elara had asked her sister the same question, only to receive a disbelieving stare.

"Dailey Cobb is the furthest thing from a bully that exists, El. If you thought about anyone besides Tripp Nightshade, you'd see that." Fury had vibrated in Payton's voice and caused it to shake. "He's hurting because I left him standing at the altar. And he has the right to be angry. Hell, you and I would be enraged if it had happened to either of us. Considering that's the first time he's seen me since then, I'd say he was pretty damned restrained."

"Payt—"

"*No!* You don't always know what's best. You only *think* you do."

Left with egg on her face, Elara had trudged back to the bookstore to comfort Florence, who hadn't been in the mood to speak to anyone and sent her home. Now, here she was, hiding like a coward. Why was everyone suddenly against her? Yes, the attention was a massive change from being ignored, but still, it hurt to be misunderstood.

Even Hex was giving her a wide berth today. Usually, he'd weave between her ankles, but the look of distaste he gave her boots was off-putting. Whenever she approached, he ran away and jumped up on the counter.

Feeling as if she'd lost her best friend, she decided to avoid people at all costs.

A knock sounded on her apartment door.

Okay, avoidance was easier said than done.

Should she ignore her visitor?

She paused in drinking her tea.

Maybe Payton was ready to forgive her?

Elara shook her head.

Doubtful. The woman could carry a grudge until doomsday, but the possibility was there, right?

With another sip, she considered her options.

If Payton *did* show up to lecture her, it would result in hurt feelings. Did she dare risk another fight with the only person in the world who once gave a crap about her?

"Elara, open the door." Tripp's tone was sweet and coaxing as if he understood her dilemma.

"It's open," she called, quickly propping her feet on the ottoman and perfecting a casual pose. No need for anyone to know she was wallowing in misery.

He wasted no time entering or surveying his surroundings, and she belatedly realized he did that a lot, acting as if he were a fugitive or feared attack from every side.

"Why do you check out a room when you enter?" Elara asked,

dropping her feet to the floor. "Like you're expecting something bad to happen?"

All expression left his face, and he gave her a blank look. A very non-Tripp expression. Whatever he was hiding, it was big.

"I want to discuss the boots," he began. "You—"

"No."

"You didn't let me finish."

"I know what you're going to say." She crossed to the sink, dumped her tea, and filled it with hot tap water to soak. When she glanced up, he was watching her with something akin to speculation. "You're going to blame every bad thing that's happened in the last couple of days on them. And I'm going to say you're wrong."

"Probably. But I'd like to tell you their origins, and you can decide how to proceed. Fair?"

How could she argue when he was reasonable? Had he been dickish, she'd have kicked him the hell out. She frowned. Maybe the boots had given her more courage than she'd thought.

"Would you like something to eat or drink first?" she offered.

"Coffee would be wonderful if it's not too much trouble." He must've recognized her dismayed gasp for what it was because he waved her off. "A glass of water would be better."

"I'm sorry. I don't stock coffee. Besides my morning latte from *Wily Witches*, the stuff makes me too jittery to drink."

He smiled, and in his gesture, she recognized an emotion close to tenderness. Her eyes suddenly stung, and she reached for a glass to hide her emotional reaction. When was the last time anyone looked at her with anything remotely like tenderness? Her dad before he disappeared?

"Ellie, you're just like your mother, my girl," he'd say.

But in reality, Payton was a free spirit like their mother, and Elara was a practical one like their father.

"Are you okay, flitter-mouse?" Tripp's concerned question interrupted her journey down memory lane.

"Fine." She handed him the water and led the way to the living room.

The instant his mouth touched the rim of the glass, her brain forgot everything but the feel of his lips on hers. Was it possible to be jealous of an inanimate object? Her body grew warm as the tip of his tongue mopped up the excess moisture, and the urge to proposition him again overcame her. If he encouraged her in any way, her thin thread of control would snap, and she'd be on him faster than a starving man attacking a loaded everything bagel.

Her sex-obsessed mind resulted from too many years without a bed buddy. It wasn't as if she didn't have opportunities, but why partake of sweet nectar when it didn't satisfy her hunger? Perfect-shouldered men were hard to find.

She curled her legs beneath her and burrowed into her favorite reading chair. The boot jewels pressed through the fabric of her favorite bohemian skirt, heating her skin, and Elara frowned. Shouldn't the amethyst stones be cool to the touch?

"What is it?" Tripp asked.

"You could stand to be a little less observant," she grumbled. "And it's nothing. Say what you're going to say, then go."

His dark brows shot up, and his lips twitched, drawing her undivided attention.

Barely suppressing a groan, she reached for his glass, downed the remaining water, and pressed the cool exterior to her feverish forehead. "Is it warm in here? It feels hot."

"It's the power of those boots, Elara. It's too strong for your body to contain." He shifted from his seat, knelt before her, and touched her thigh. "I'm begging you. Take them off."

"You keep saying that, but they're just boots, Tripp. There's nothing magical about them other than how gorgeous they are."

"Yesterday, you effortlessly cast a spell in the alleyway. Whether you choose to believe it or not, you set fire to that box in the bookstore." His fingers tightened when she would've protested. "You asked me how old I am. Old enough to have seen what these things can do. To recognize their signature in any room I walk into."

"I didn't start that fire, Tripp. I wasn't there and wouldn't do that to Florence."

"I'm not saying you would, but are you sure you weren't in the store's proximity in the minutes before the blaze?"

"Positive."

The pressure of his fingers wasn't great, yet it was all she could feel through the skirt's fabric. Like the jewels, his touch created a heat verging on burning, and Elara squirmed.

She focused on his mouth, recalling how incredible their kisses were and the passion they stirred. The temptation to experience more was mighty, as was her desire to discover if he always tasted of brownies and espresso. The air filled with the scent of baked chocolate delicacies, and Elara leaned forward, eager to find the source.

Her face connected with his palm, and she sputtered her indignation. His dimples flashed, irritating her further.

"What's so freaking funny?" she snapped.

"Your face when you don't get what you want," he said, chuckling.

She toyed with the idea of rearranging his.

Tripp dropped a kiss on her nose, which Elara immediately scrubbed away.

"Don't be mad, flitter-mouse. If or when we make love, I can promise you won't be wearing those fucking boots."

"Or maybe I will because I love them, and you still haven't told me why you believe they're the worst thing since raisins in cookies." She crossed her arms and sat back. "Let's hear it."

"You don't like raisins in cookies?" he asked, distracted.

"No. Hate them. I always mistake them for chocolate chip and wind up disappointed." Yes, she was grouchy, but nothing was worse than having an itch for one man who refused to scratch it. "Your reason for hating my boots. Go."

CHAPTER NINE

Elara was infuriating!

But Tripp would be damned if he let his annoyance show. Teasing her had been a surefire way to rile her and remove the too-tempting desire from her eyes. And thank the ancestors, she'd missed the reference to making love. How such romantic drivel had poured out of his mouth, he'd never know. Sex was sex, and he ran from entanglements. In the future, should he consider a long-term liaison, it couldn't be with a mortal. That way lay death for said mortal. The Gods enjoyed throwing hurdles in lovers' paths, and many never survived the trials heaped on them.

Tripp made the mistake of locking eyes with Elara.

She possessed a rare vulnerability. Insecurity and the need to be taken seriously were paramount for her. But beneath those, she desired to be wild and wicked, as she believed her sister was. Payton wasn't. Oh, she put on a decent act, and it seemed the ignorant people in Witchmere fell for it. Yet Payton Hawthorne was steadfast and as equally messed up in her beliefs as Elara. It came down to absentee parents and a grandmother who refused to tell them about their connection.

"Come here, flitter-mouse," Tripp urged softly. Surprised that she complied, he tucked her against his chest and rested his cheek on her glossy ash-blonde hair. Those shiny locks were as silky as they looked, and he luxuriated in the feel. "Let me tell you the story of the boots."

"They first showed up as a pair of ankle-tie sandals. I believe you would call them gladiator sandals today," he said. "They appeared right before the eruption of Mount Vesuvius in the ancient city of Pompeii."

"Wait, what?" She drew away and frowned up at him. "There's no way they can magically transform, but even if they *could*, they can't be that old. *You* can't be that old."

"They are. I'm not."

"Tripp." Her tone was admonishing, indicating she didn't believe a word.

Pressing his finger to her pillowy-soft lips, and heaving an internal groan at the delightful feel, he shushed her. "Let me finish the story, Elara."

Although she grimaced, she rested her cheek against his chest. "Fine."

He fought a grin, lost, and immediately scowled. When he opened his arms to her, he hadn't considered how right she'd feel or how inviting her spring-meadow scent would be, tempting him to roll about in her garden.

Tripp shook his head to clear it.

Get it together, Tripp!

"Where was I?" he mused aloud.

"Mount Vesuvius."

"Right." He kissed her temple, unable to help himself. "They appeared right before the eruption as a gift from a jilted suitor to my mother. He happened to be a Trickster."

"What's a Trickster?"

"You'd know them as the Norse God, Loki, and the Greek God, Hermes. The last one is considered the Divine Trickster, but I suspect another created those shoes."

"Who is your mother, and how did she run afoul of deities?"

"She's the Goddess Brelenia of Messia," Tripp confessed.

Elara stiffened in his arms, and he waited for her to process what he'd told her. Expecting protest or, at the very least, a disbelieving scoff, he was somewhat surprised when she relaxed against him and said, "Yeah, it makes sense."

"What does? That my mother is a deity?" he asked.

"Yes. I mean, *look* at you."

Her fingers had found the bare skin underneath his sweater and traced the ridges of his abdomen. His body's reaction was immediate, and Tripp conjugated verbs to calm his cock's response. Unfortunately, the ones he'd chosen were all sexual acts, which gave the *root* of those verbs a different meaning.

"Tell her to stop, Tripp. Tell her to stop right now!" his wiser side counseled.

But her caresses felt divine, and he'd been without a woman's touch for far too long.

"What was another kiss between friends, Tripp?" his devilish side asked.

Pressing his fingertips to her jaw, he repositioned her head and lowered his. An instant before his mouth claimed hers, a furious, flying furball hit him mid back, yowling loud enough to wake the dead. Or scare the living into an early grave!

"Hex! No!"

Before Tripp could send the evil spawn to Hades, where it belonged, Elara plucked it from his back. When his gaze locked with the cat's, his gut clenched, and he choked on his outrage.

"Where did you get that thing?" he demanded hoarsely, surging to his feet.

"Hex?"

"Yes," he ground out between clenched teeth.

"He showed up behind the building one day, looking sad. When I couldn't find a microchip, I scryed for his home, but it only showed the local graveyard." Elara rubbed her cheek against the beast's puffed-up fur. "I figured his previous owner must've died recently."

"Elara, that's no ordinary cat."

She drew back and frowned at the faux-animal's suddenly innocent-looking face. "Yes, he is. He even had a collar. That's how I knew his name was Hex. Although why anyone would carve his name in the tag but not add a phone number makes no sense to me."

"Did you keep it? The collar?"

Since Tripp couldn't see anything but rhinestones glued to black nylon, he assumed not, but he had to ask. He needed to see the symbol on the back of the band if it existed.

After kissing Hex's head, she set him on the chair and went to the kitchen. He never wanted to rush someone so badly. While she was gone, Tripp knelt beside the beast and leaned in.

"I know what you are, Trickster. If you hurt her in any way, I'll rip your insides out," he warned in a low voice. "Excruciatingly slow."

The furball had the audacity to wink.

"Transform back into your standard human form and show her what you are," he ordered.

The sour expression on its face gave him pause. Powerful magic was required to trap a Trickster. Yet, now he thought about it more, the spell should've been broken the instant the collar was removed, so why wasn't it? Was it possible the enchantment wasn't contained in the object but in the animal itself?

Mother might be able to provide insight.

"Here." Elara handed him the leather band with a gold disc.

Etched in the front was the single word "Hex." Careful not to touch the metal, Tripp turned the band inside out and held it to the light. The symbols were some of the oldest he'd encountered. Removing his phone, he snapped a picture and returned the collar to Elara. If she'd handled it in the past, she was immune.

"Hex isn't his name, Elara. The word is intended to warn those who come in contact with that beastly thing."

"Come on, Tripp. I'd know if he wasn't a standard stray."

She loved the thing and wouldn't be swayed by the truth. More proof was needed before Tripp removed the Trickster from her home.

"How long have you had the, uh, *cat?*" he asked.

"As long as I've lived here, just under three years or so. He's indoor-outdoor, but he always returns for the night."

I'll bet he does. He told himself it wasn't the cat he was jealous of—it was the Trickster whom she cuddled.

Elara tossed the collar onto the table, sending Hex bolting from the room.

"Hm. Maybe we should keep that handy so your bloody cat avoids us during our more intimate moments," Tripp suggested.

Elara's comely blush lifted his mood.

"Yeah, it seems we're cursed," she muttered. "Or I am, at least."

"No, flitter-mouse, just those boots." He tucked a strand of her hair behind her delicate ear. "They've been responsible for a high percentage of the world's disasters, natural and man-made."

"That's ridiculous, Tripp. No single pair of boots, however pretty, can cause all that."

"It's true," he replied flatly. "Despite their chaos, Mother found her true love, my father. Unfortunately, she believed in passing on her good fortune."

"You aren't interested in finding true love?" Elara's expression was downcast, and she'd be mortified if she knew her feelings were on display. Although his first impulse was to reassure her, Tripp couldn't. He wasn't positive he believed in unfailing affection or that it was meant to last forever, as gods—or demigods, in his case—were wont to live.

"No. Whenever I show the slightest interest in someone, Mother adds her fatal footwear into the mix. Disaster follows."

"You said natural and man-made. How is that possible?" she asked, distancing herself and curling into the chair as if attempting to make herself smaller.

Again, the impulse to comfort her was intense. He hated her withdrawal, but it was for the best. Her air of disbelief annoyed him enough to maintain his space. If the Gods were kind, she'd be tearing those fucking boots off her feet by now, but life was never so easy.

Sighing, he sat across from her.

"The first woman I truly cared for was in London, England. I was twenty-five in mortal years and quite full of myself. It was late summer sixteen-sixty-six when I saw her at the market." Odd, but he could no longer recall the woman's name. Elara's engaging blue eyes, ash-blonde hair, and shy manner were reminiscent of the young maid, though, and the sight of her rapt attention caused his heart to constrict. "After a few weeks of courtship, I made the mistake of telling my mother I wished to remove the girl from her life of drudgery and bring her to Messia." Tripp shook his head. "Mother forwarded the cursed shoes as silk slippers with ruby rosettes, not realizing they were too rich for a servant to possess and would find her in trouble as a suspected thief. Those shoes sparked the Great London Fire in Thomas Farriner's bakery that fateful night in September."

Elara's mouth hung slightly ajar, and she stared at him in wonder. "How?"

"Her employer, Farriner, discovered the bejeweled slippers and locked her in the pantry, believing the maid had stolen them from one of the upstanding citizens he did business with. His daughter was sent to fetch the constable, but stumbling around in the dark shop, she set it ablaze."

"What happened to the maid?"

"She perished in the fire, though Farriner, his son, and his flighty daughter made good their escape."

With her hands pressed to her mouth, Elara released a distressed cry that Tripp felt to his soul. Or maybe it was the remembered grief of his loss.

"Oh, Tripp! I'm so sorry." Reaching across the side table, she gripped his hand. "Truly."

"It was a long time ago," he said, brushing aside her kindness.

Once again, the maid's large, expressive eyes flashed through his mind. She and Elara looked so similar that they could be sisters. Was that his attraction for Elara? Had her resemblance to his lover triggered his memory and made him experience a fondness he wouldn't otherwise feel? It bore further consideration.

"Are you okay?" she asked softly.

Her face superimposed over the maid's, and recognition struck him. With a nagging suspicion, he lifted her left hand, brushed back her sleeve, and checked inside her elbow. Not expecting to find his lover's birthmark, Tripp swore when he saw it. Shaped like a kidney bean, it was two shades darker than her usual skin tone.

Just like...

Elaina.

The name drifted through his mind along with the memory of what he'd called her.

Flitter-mouse.

He dropped Elara's arm and leaped to his feet. "I must go."

"Tripp? What's wrong?"

How did one broach the subject to a potential lover that she was a replica of another woman he'd once held affection for?

They didn't. Not if he ever expected to spend time in her bed.

The eerie feeling of being watched skated along his skin, and Tripp glanced through her bedroom doorway. Hex appeared superior and satisfied by the unfolding events, the little shit.

"Tripp?" Elara rose and placed her hand on his chest. "Talk to me. What's wrong?"

"Those goddamned boots," he snarled. "Get rid of them, Elara. The sooner, the better."

Like the veriest coward, he raced for the closest exit. Then, realizing he wasn't on the first floor, Tripp pivoted away from the deck slider and stalked to the apartment door.

"I mean it."

CHAPTER TEN

Tripp Nightshade.

That arrogant bastard!

Two days had passed since he stormed out of Elara's apartment with his stupid dictate to get rid of her precious boots. Everywhere she looked, he was lurking around corners, ducking away if she made eye contact, and running for the closest exit.

Much the way she had reacted to him until recently.

The irony wasn't lost on her.

It would be funny if it weren't pathetic. The man believed he was the son of a deity. Initially, his claim felt, well, *right* somehow. It justified those otherworldly looks and his undeniable magnetism for anyone from birth to death. It also explained why every time they kissed, the heavens rumbled, the ground shook beneath their feet, and the eternal call of love echoed within their souls, urging them on.

Or maybe those things only happened to her.

Maybe he hadn't felt anything at all.

And wasn't *that* depressing?

Elara released the dumpster's lid and jumped when it clanked. The stupid sound was a death knell for her love life.

Again, depressing.

Cigarette smoke drifted to her as a perfectly rounded O, and she shifted to face the *Never Too Many* bookstore owner. Florence watched her through narrowed eyes as if trying to determine what was different about her lately.

Elara wanted to give her a fist bump and shout, "I kissed Tripp Nightshade," but it was doubtful Old Flo would approve.

Usually, she'd ask, "Shouldn't you give those things up, Flo?" But today, she didn't have the heart. Instead, she stole the home-rolled cigarette from the older woman, placed it between her lips, and inhaled like a pro. The coughing fit caused her employer to cackle, but Elara got the last laugh by snuffing it out under her booted foot.

"Cancer sticks," she snapped.

"Not for witches, gel," Florence replied with a smile resembling fondness. Her shrewd eyes missed nothing as they passed over Elara's face. "Want to talk about it?"

"It?" she asked, stalling for time.

"Yes. *It*. Your misery over that ridiculous demigod."

"You know?" Why she was surprised, Elara couldn't say. Flo's network was vast, and she ferreted out everything before long. She was Witchmere's version of the CIA, MI6, and Interpol combined.

"Pfft! The entire town is watching the two of you dance around your attraction. What's not to know?"

Elara groaned in dismay. The desire to hide inside her apartment for the next thirty years was intense. "I need to move somewhere no one knows me. Like Siberia."

"You speak Russian?"

"No, but I can learn."

Florence produced another misshapen cigarette, noted Elara's squint-eyed stare, and shrugged. "You think I don't know it's a nasty habit, gel? They calm my nerves."

"You never seem to be upset," Elara replied.

"Because I smoke." After lighting her second cigarette,

Florence inhaled deeply and closed her eyes. "You should protect yourself. Sleep with Enguerrand if you must, but don't lose your heart to him."

"Who is Enguerrand?"

With a laugh, her boss stubbed out the tip of the just-lit cigarette, shoved it into her cardigan, and turned to leave.

"Flo!"

She paused and glanced over her shoulder.

Elara held up her hands. "Who is Enguerrand? You've mentioned him twice."

"It's your man's real name, gel. Enguerrand the Third of Messia." She narrowed her eyes and tipped her head. "Perhaps you should learn more about a fella before you jump into bed with him, yeah?"

Having delivered those wise words, Florence abandoned Elara to her self-doubts and recriminations.

"Enguerrand the Third of Messia," she murmured. "*Tripp.* Of course."

"I've always hated the name Enguerrand," he said softly.

Elara spun with a gasp, then immediately scowled. "Didn't anyone ever teach you not to sneak up on unsuspecting females in dark alleys?" she snapped.

Deep grooves appeared on his cheeks as he grinned. "It's actually in the demigod handbook. Dark alleys are the absolute best place to find unsuspecting females."

"Whatever." Remembering she was irritated at his evasiveness, she waved him off and headed for the bookstore. Right before she reached the knob, he wedged his way between her and the door.

"I'm sorry, Elara," he said solemnly.

"For?" she asked, dragging it out, not necessarily ready to forgive without him being properly repentant.

"For my abhorrent behavior the other day and for avoiding you ever since." He tucked a lock of her windblown hair behind her ear. The warmth of his touch chased the winter chill from her skin. "You should wear a hat on cold nights like tonight."

"I'm fine." And she was. Mainly because he was showering her with the attention she'd always craved. Warmth swelled in her chest. "And I forgive you for your abhorrent behavior."

"But not for avoiding you?" he teased.

Scrunching her nose, she shook her head. "No need for you to apologize in that regard. I avoid you all the time."

He shifted closer and touched his nose to hers, and her breath caught in her throat.

"For which *you* should apologize to *me*, flitter-mouse."

A wave of amorous energy swept up from the boots, crashing over her. Elara wrapped her arms around his neck and used one hand to drag his face down, close to her lips.

"Mm. No. I don't think I will."

Then, she initiated their kiss. And miracle of miracles, he responded by encircling her waist with one of those steel bands he called arms and weaving his fingers into her hair to tilt her head back. Their kiss was beyond steamy, and she leaped upward, hugging his hips with her thighs. He shifted to support her weight, not breaking contact with her mouth, and Elara moaned her pleasure as she pressed into him.

As she broke to drag air into her lungs, she spotted Bohdan Sanderson's grinning face a few feet away.

"I know you're there, Sanderson," Tripp said. "But you're getting better."

"You only know because she saw me," Bodhan retorted. "Sloppy, man. Real sloppy."

"Remind me to have you tied and your furry ass waxed during the next full moon for interrupting an intimate moment," Tripp said with an evil grin.

The wolf shifter paled. "I only came to tell you that the countdown has started. You don't have to be a dick about it."

"You know what to do." Tripp stared down at her, and Elara initially believed he was speaking to her until he called over his shoulder, "We'll be there in an hour."

"I'll tell the others." Wraith-like, Bohdan disappeared into the shadows.

"I don't know what that was all about, but your threat was genius," Elara said, nodding her approval. "Pure genius."

"I've been around a good while and had plenty of time to devise clever punishments for the wicked."

All her girl parts tingled, and she clamped her lips together to keep from panting. Why did his comment sound sexual? Was that her overheated mind and under-pleasured body?

Florence's words returned to her. *"Perhaps you should learn more about a fella before you jump into bed with him, yeah?"*

With an abundance of regret, Elara unlocked her legs and slid down his body. Watching for any signs of falsehood, she asked, "Is your mother truly a goddess?"

Other than a grimace of distaste, he appeared truthful when he said, "Yes."

"Why does it bother you?"

Instead of answering, he clasped her hand. "I'll tell you another time. First, I must finish explaining the problem with those boots, Elara."

"Why can't you give it a rest, Tripp? Nothing dire has happened in the last four days."

"Did you not hear Bohdan say the countdown had begun?"

She had, but the blood pounding in her ears from their mini-makeout had quieted any questions she may have had, and her brain cells weren't working in unison quite yet.

After giving herself a mental scolding, she said, "Explain, please."

"I will." Raising her hand, he kissed the inside of her wrist. "Let's get a bite to eat, and I'll tell you what I know."

"Let me tell Flo I'm leaving."

Tripp was delaying the inevitable. It might've been the fact that Elara had felt too good in his arms or that avoiding her had seemed like torture. Perhaps not as agonizing as when he'd waited on news of Elaina's fate after the fire or as difficult as the times he'd had to avert disaster in his past, but the last few days ranked up there.

His mother had conveniently disappeared, and no amount of scrying produced her whereabouts. Once again, she'd left him to clean up her mess. And things in Witchmere were about to get messy. The mountain had begun rumbling the day Elara tried on the boots, and the quakes had progressed up the Richter scale. The heightened seismic activity could only mean Rainier would blow her top, and soon, if he didn't find a way to prevent it. Instead of snow this holiday season, fire and ash would rain down on everyone.

Once seated in a booth at *Serendipity*—the quaint soup shop owned and operated by yet another Sanderson—Tripp entwined his fingers with Elara's atop the table. Although he was never one to care what others thought, he did, however, care about her comfort.

"Is this okay, flitter-mouse?"

"Holding hands like a couple of teenagers?" she asked. Her voice was breathy, and the restaurant's low light couldn't hide her charming flush of color.

"Yes." What would she have been like as a teen? Responsible, he imagined. She'd have felt the need for stability and would've smothered her desire to act out or behave as a normal kid might've.

Elara nodded, keeping her gaze locked on their joined hands. "It's okay."

"You're sure?" he prodded, giving a gentle shake to gain her attention.

Turning those overbright eyes to him, she nodded. "I'm sure."

Tripp should've been concerned by the blatant adoration or felt uneasy at the very least, but his reaction was the opposite.

Maybe the secluded atmosphere lent to the intimacy he was caught up in because he didn't want to break the enchanting romantic spell surrounding them. Their meal couldn't be called a date, but it felt like one.

He hated to ruin it.

Elara's expression turned wary. "What is it, Tripp?"

And wasn't it odd she could read him better than his own family?

Just like Elaina.

"I find myself drawn to you more than I should be," he confessed. "It never ends well for the lover of a god or demigod. I don't want you to be a casualty of the Fates' whims."

Her fingers tightened in his. "Are you positive I will be?"

Yes.

But he couldn't voice it. Couldn't bring himself to destroy her bubble of security. If he were a weaker man, he'd walk away, but he had boots to destroy and a volcano to tame.

As he opened his mouth, Katie Sanderson approached, giving their clasped hands a curious look and him an open, flirty smile. If she hadn't been as friendly with Elara, he'd have left and never frequented her shop again.

"Hello, you two! I see the rumors are true." She winked at Elara. "Well done, you!"

"People should mind their own business." Tripp's reply was sharp, and his look pointed. "Did anyone ever consider *I'm* the lucky one who caught *her*?"

Both women sucked in a breath and stared at him in shocked wonder. His outburst surprised him, too.

Katie was the first to recover, giving him a broad smile. "Well done, *you*, Tripp Nightshade! And not just for catching Elara, but for recognizing her worth." Leaning in, she kissed Elara's cheek. "He's a keeper, hon."

"So is she," he said in a soft voice.

"Oh, I know. It's the stupid men of this town who can't see beyond the end of their noses."

"Or they've been warned off," Archer Roche said as he approached.

The women gaped at him, and heat rode Tripp's cheeks.

"I never did that," he denied hotly.

"You did. Not with words, but your warning looks promised retribution."

Archer's smirk irked, and Tripp longed to wipe it off the man's face. But Elara's sigh bubbled with happiness, improving his mood. Not one hundred percent because they were inundated with townsfolk when he wanted to be alone, but enough that the violent urge to add Archer's head to Mount Rushmore had lessened.

"Why are you here, Roche?" he asked. "Can I not have five minutes alone with Elara without someone up my ass?"

"Bohdan wanted me to tell you about the latest reading and the frequency of quakes."

All the ancient curses he'd learned were on the tip of his tongue, but his mother would cut it out if he voiced them in front of the women. With Witchmere magically protected as she was, the town would only feel the worst of the earthquakes, which started with Elara happily parading about in those purple plagues on her feet.

"How long do we have?" he asked.

"Based on his calculations, four days. Five at the most."

"So, enough time for us to dine before the meeting?" Tripp asked pointedly.

"Yeah. Sorry."

"No problem, but tell Bohdan that Rowen is heating her wax pot."

CHAPTER ELEVEN

Tripp Nightshade.

Elara was sharing an honest-to-god meal with Tripp Nightshade. She'd like to say the memory would be etched in her mind forever, but other than shamelessly watching him consume focaccia, she couldn't recall what they'd been served.

"You're not listening, flitter-mouse," he admonished.

"No," she admitted. "Sorry. What were you saying?"

Pushing aside his bowl, he shifted to face her, cocking up a leg and draping his arm along the booth seat. She nearly swooned at the sexy, casual pose. Was he aware of the picture he made?

"I swear I'll pay attention this time," she lied, crossing her index finger over her heart.

His dimples flashed, and his eyes crinkled. "Doubtful. Where did your mind wander?"

Heat crept up her chest and into her face. "That's best not said in polite company."

"There'll be time for that when we destroy the boots, Elara." He tipped up her chin. "I need you to hear me."

"Go on," she urged, hoping he'd abandon his foolish plan.

"I was telling you about the French Revolution and, more importantly, about Élise."

Right. Another ex-lover.

Elara tried to quell the building jealousy, but his every story began with some female he'd been hot for, who was gifted a pair of shoes or boots like hers. This idea of shoes magically transforming was preposterous, but she let him drone on, hoping to get to the good part, when they would become lovers, like the other women.

She sipped her red wine and nodded in sympathy as he told the tale of Élise's death. And when he spoke of Bonaparte, she showed the appropriate outrage. Glancing over his shoulder, she noted the time.

"Didn't you tell Archer and Bohdan you would join them soon?"

His expression arrested. "Are you trying to get rid of me?"

Busted.

"No. But this conversation is going nowhere, and I have to return to the bookstore. It's only five days until Christmas, and I can't leave Flo in a lurch."

"Elara!"

She set her wine glass on the table with a sigh. "I love my purple boots, Tripp. They're the most comfortable pair I've ever owned, and they're gorgeous. I've worn them for over four days, and I feel fine. Not a single desire to burn down a city or start a revolution."

"You're not taking this seriously."

"And you're taking it *too* seriously." She slid from the booth. "I've got to go. Do you want me to cover half the bill?"

His face was the stuff of thunderstorms. Dark and stormy, ready to shoot lightning bolts in every direction.

She blinked.

Maybe he was related to Zeus, after all.

"No, I don't want you to pay," he replied in a clipped voice. "I've got it."

"Thanks." With anyone else, she might've leaned in to kiss their cheek or, if they were dating, their lips. But his fury was off-putting, and she scurried away like the flitter-mouse he called her.

Just as she opened the door, he gripped the edge above her head, holding it in place. "We aren't done with this conversation, Elara Hawthorne. Those boots are dangerous, and I won't stop until you recognize it."

"Yeah, okay. Talk soon." With a wave, she ducked under his arm and hurried away. But every time she glanced over her shoulder, he was there, keeping pace to the bookstore. Granted, Witchmere was the size of a postage stamp, but still, it was intimidating.

Probably what he intended.

Elara was made of sterner stuff, and his tactics wouldn't work on her. Much.

When she arrived at *Never Too Many*, business was booming, and it seemed half the townspeople mingled among the tourists. As far as she was concerned, books were the perfect gifts, but tonight was the busiest the store had ever been.

"Get over here, Elara," Florence ordered with a scowl. "Where did you run off to? Can't you see we're as busy as one-armed paper hangers?"

"You mean your network of spies didn't tell you?" she countered, tying on the pine-green logoed apron that made her skin look sallow. If she were the owner, she'd change them to a bright, cheerful pink. "And not for nothing, but I told you I was taking a break. Those are required by law."

"Sass is not appropriate in a business setting, gel."

"And yet yours is constant," Payton said with an eye roll and a slap of novels on the counter. "These are for Mrs. Everett, and you're about to be late for your meeting, Flo."

"Yes." Eyeing the crowded room with concern, she glanced between Elara and Payton. "Can you gels handle the rush?"

"Go," Payton urged in a less challenging tone. "We won't let you down."

For once, Flo didn't respond with snark as she patted Payton's hand. "Thank you."

"What the hell is going on, Pay?" Elara asked after she'd left. "Why is everyone acting all shady and shit?"

"Who's everyone?"

"Tripp, Flo, Archer Roche, and Bohdan Sanderson." She paused and smiled at Mrs. Everett as the petite, gray-haired woman approached. "Would you like these gift-wrapped, ma'am?"

"No, dear. I have no one left to share the holiday with. Those are for me."

Elara shared a sad look with her sister. Mrs. Everett's comment represented their worst fear: dying alone with no one to care what happened to them. She wanted to gather the frail older woman close and promise to cook her the best holiday feast known to man. The only problem? She couldn't boil water without scorching a pan.

"I recognize that look, dear, but don't you worry about me," Mrs. Everett told her. "I've had a wonderful life, full of love and laughter."

Payton smiled and skirted the counter with the bag of books. "Let me take these to your car for you."

"Thank you, sweet Payton, but I walked here. I'd like Elara to escort me home if you don't mind. She lives close to me."

Elara shot her sister a panicked glance. Errand Girl wasn't high on the list of skills she wanted on her resumé, but how did she deny the request when it was phrased so nicely? "If you can wait until the rush ends, I'd be happy to, Mrs. Everett," she finally said with a resigned sigh.

The woman glanced around as if just noticing the crowd. A slight frown marred her brow, and her eyes appeared distressed. "Oh, my."

"I'll tell you what. How about I make you a nice cup of tea, and you wait in the reading area with one of your new books?" Payton suggested, wrapping an arm around the petite woman's shoulders.

"I promise, it's no bother at all," she added, cutting through an apologetic protest.

Elara marveled for the millionth time at how easily her sister handled people. Her unique brand of charm and million-watt smile got her whatever she wanted.

Except for approval from Mayor Cobb.

Speak of the Devil...

The sour-faced woman was next in line, and her glare spoke volumes. "When did Payton return to town?"

"This week." Elara accepted the stack of hardbacks and began scanning the barcodes. "Will there be anything else for you today, Mayor?" she asked, accepting her credit card.

"Not unless you can send that girl back under the rock she crawled from."

Fury exploded in Elara's brain. This snobby twatasaurus was the reason for her sister's unhappiness! Mary-Alice Cobb had some freaking nerve coming into Payton's place of employment and starting her special brand of stinky-ass shit!

Whipping out Flo's sharpest pair of shears, Elara cut the Mayor's card in two.

"Declined!" she snapped.

"What?"

"Yeah, sorry. Looks like you're overdrawn," Elara declared in a ringing voice, making sure the customers at the end of the line heard. *"That's* embarrassing, huh, *Mayor?"*

"You little bi—"

"Careful," Tripp warned from behind Elara.

She squeaked her surprise, like the mouse he'd nicknamed her. His arm encircled her waist in a protective gesture as he leaned toward Payton's nemesis.

"Insulting her insults me, Mayor," he said in a silky tone. "I promise you, you do *not* want to do that."

But Mary-Alice refused to be cowed and sneered her disgust. "Mark my words, Tripp Nightshade. You'll come to regret defending those good-for-nothing Hawthornes."

"Doubtful," he snapped.

Lightning flashed, and thunder boomed loud enough to vibrate the floor. The windows rattled, and the overhead chandeliers swayed.

From the corner of her eye, Elara detected movement. She waited until the Mayor sped on her way before she looked that way.

Dailey Cobb was resting a shoulder against the bookcase. With his thumbs tucked into his utility belt and booted feet crossed at the ankles, he appeared to be an indolent officer without a care in the world despite witnessing the confrontation with his mother.

The cold-eyed stare he graced her with sent a chill along her spine.

"That goes for you, too, Cobb," Tripp said, shifting to stand between them. "The Hawthornes are under my protection."

"Noted, Mr. Demigod," Dailey replied with a mocking twist of his lips.

Fuck.

Word had spread about what Tripp was, and challenges would pour in soon, as they did wherever he landed. As a demigod, he was the top dog in town, and all the other wannabe alphas were quick to pick a fight they couldn't win. As a hella-powerful warlock, Dailey Cobb might become a major problem.

The urge to ask if he'd been the one to produce the thunderous display was strong, but Tripp let it go. He'd discover the cause in due time.

In his distraction, he'd forgotten Elara's fighting spirit was enhanced by the dreaded boots, and he wasn't prepared for her shove. He almost fell into the credenza, doubling as a gift-wrapping station behind the counter.

"I'm sorry about your mother, Dailey," she said, charging forward and slapping the mutilated credit card in the officer's hands. "But if either of you thinks you're going to harass my sister, you're grossly mistaken."

"Hm. Maybe I dated the wrong Hawthorne," he drawled.

The comment detonated a rage bomb inside Tripp's head. This time, he was the one who produced the elemental shit-storm. The overhead lights flashed, thunder boomed, and the bookshelves rocked precariously.

"Rein it in, Enguerrand," Florence said, sidling up to him. "And get your arse over to the meeting." She held up a hand. "Don't worry, I'll escort Dailey myself. But if you boys believe for one second that I'll allow fighting in my store, magical or otherwise, you've another think coming. Understood?"

"But El—"

"In case you missed it, Elara has a spine of steel," Payton assured him as she joined their small group and accepted books from the next wide-eyed customer in line. "Hello, Mr. Caldwell. Will there be anything else today? No? How is Mrs. Caldwell?"

Tripp looked at Elara with new eyes.

His girl possessed a fire in her soul, and her hands were balled into fists as she stalked back to the counter. "I thought you had somewhere to be, Flo. I told you Payton and I could handle things here."

"And I believed ya, gel, but when the Mayor accosted me on the street and threatened to shut down my shop, I thought it was best to return."

"She did *what?*" Payton shoved Caldwell's purchase into his hands with more force than necessary and slammed the register drawer. "That miserable cow! What I wouldn't give to turn her into a toad!"

Elara nodded. "We should—"

Clapping a hand over her mouth, Tripp responded with a vehement shake of his head.

"Don't even think it, Elara." Placing his mouth next to her ear, he lowered his voice and said, "Remember the boots, flitter-mouse. A Trickster conjured them if you recall, and you'll be unable to remove any curse you create while they're on your feet."

Peeling his fingers away, she glared.

"I don't like being controlled, Tripp Nightshade, and I'll advise you to knock it off," she growled.

Florence and Payton wore equally challenging expressions, causing him to throw up his hands in defeat.

"Teach her about consequences, Florence," he warned. "It's your job, now."

"She already understands, and if you truly knew anything about her, you'd see she's a responsible adult." Florence thumped his chest. "Get yourself and that mama's boy out of my shop. Neither of you had better set foot in here again until you've learned to show respect for my granddaughters."

Tripp's jaw sagged, not from the challenge itself but because of her slip.

Dailey shifted forward as he registered Payton's shock, but Tripp's pot of give-a-shit-about-anyone-but-Elara was on the back burner, and he held up a hand to halt Dailey's progress.

Tears filled Elara's wide china-blue eyes as she gaped at Florence. "Why didn't you tell us?"

The store grew silent as everyone held their collective breath, waiting for the answer.

"I wanted to," Florence confessed hoarsely. "So many times I started to tell you, but I…" She shook her head in despair.

Unable and unwilling to let others witness their pain, Tripp snapped his fingers, freezing the entire room except for the Hawthornes and Florence.

"Now's not the time," he warned gently. "The gawkers—"

"I don't give a flea on a rat's ass what these people think," Florence snapped. "I never did. I only care about my gels."

"If you cared so damned much, why didn't you say something?" Payton cried. "You had *years* to find us—in addition to the three we were here!"

"I didn't want you to hate me for causing your parents' disappearance," she confessed.

Tripp's heart ached for her. "You aren't to blame. You never were."

CHAPTER TWELVE

From her corner of the bookshop, Brelenia observed her son's interactions with the mortals. Whether he cared to admit it or not, he loved Elara. She hadn't been worthy in her incarnations as Elaina, Élise, or any other woman Tripp had been attracted to. But now, the girl stood a fighting chance. For the first time in history, Elara ruled the boots, not vice versa.

No, the current problem was Enguerrand's battle-scarred heart. If he didn't stop causing earthquakes and bookstore fires with his intense emotions, Mt. Rainier would blow, and it wouldn't be a minor eruption. It would be as epic as Pompeii.

"Nice disguise, Brelenia of Messia," a deep, amused voice said beside her. She didn't need to look up to know who was there.

"Hello, Hermes."

"Does my cousin still believe those boots were created by any old Trickster?" he asked casually.

Brelenia did glance at him then. "I told him they were a gift from a jilted suitor."

Hermes chuckled and took the seat opposite her.

"What are you doing here?" she asked, curious what he was about all these years later.

Based on his black, close-cropped hair and beard, the modern cold-weather clothing, and superior air, he was attempting to pass as a mortal in the small town of Witchmere.

"Same as you, I imagine." Unbuttoning his navy pea coat, he crossed his legs and poured himself a spot of tea. Although he sipped from the delicate cup, he didn't look ridiculous, as one might expect of an uber-masculine male.

"You seem at home among mortals," she said.

He snorted a laugh, and his emerald eyes twinkled. "And no one would guess you're not a frail old woman who has 'no one left to share the holiday with.'"

"Mrs. Everett was a well-respected citizen of this town, I'll have you know." Brelenia grinned. "And I appreciate the use of her body now that she's transitioned to the next world."

"The meat suit is borrowed?" Hermes's dark brows shot up. "Considering you're a goddess, one would assume you'd glamour."

She shuddered. "Must you be crass? 'Meat suit' is such an ugly term. As an advocate of humans, I would think you'd be kinder."

"Apologies, love." His grin belied any contrived contriteness. Glancing at the cast of players in Tripp's drama, his gaze sharpened. "Who's the blonde?"

"Elara. She's meant for Enguerrand, so don't interfere," she warned.

"No, I'm familiar with her. Who is the other one behind Florence Shaw?"

"Elara's sister and she's also off limits to you. Payton is meant for the stubborn warlock in the uniform."

It was Hermes's turn to shudder. "A warlock? Seriously? The girl could do better."

"Like you, for example?"

"For example."

Brelenia laughed. "They're going through a rough patch at the moment. I don't believe they are meant to reconcile for at *least* another year, in case you wish to show her a good time. However, don't either of you fall in love. That way lies tragedy, dear boy."

"I don't fall into feelings, as well you know."

His words held an edge, and her heart pinged. "You'll get over your heartache one day, Hermes. I promise you."

"I'm over it now. As the enchanted shoes attested, you and your mortal were always meant to be. He passed the tests." His sad eyes locked with hers, and there was longing in their depths. "You were never like the rest of us, Brel. Perhaps that's what made you more attractive to me than anyone else."

"But I don't subscribe to inter-family relationships, as you know. And having seen you in nappies, knowing you're not well endowed, I'm not interested," she teased, hoping to lighten the mood.

As the son of her brother Zeus, Hermes would never win her as a lover. Brelenia spoke the truth. All the incestuous relationships between the Gods and royalty made her physically ill.

"Besides, dear boy, our kind is already inbred enough, and half are mad."

"Yes." Pasting on a game smile, he stole a cookie from her plate and examined it. "That's precisely why I intend to take a page from your book and look elsewhere for love, should I ever desire to feel my heart crushed again."

She laughed as he intended she should. "And in the meantime?"

"I'll watch you torture your son with enchanted footwear," he quipped with a wicked grin.

Brelenia narrowed her eyes. "What did you do, Hermes?"

"Nothing."

"Why don't I believe you?" she asked dryly, raising a stern brow.

"Because you're supremely untrusting, love."

"Fair." She turned her gaze back to her son's drama, confident she appeared suspended like the Witchmere residents. Hermes was visible only to her or Enguerrand, should he happen to glance their way. "What are their chances this time, do you suppose?"

"The stakes are higher."

Her heart rate increased. "How so?"

"Rainier is active beneath the Earth's crust. It won't take much for them to trigger it."

Just as she suspected!

"Like Pompeii?" she clarified.

"Yes."

"And Witchmere will be lost?"

"Along with this entire corner of North America."

"What did you do, Hermes? How can we help them succeed?"

"It's why I'm here. This is their final chance, Brel. Either they get it right, or the mountain blows." He covered her hand and squeezed. "I didn't alter the boots. Tripp and Elara did that, causing them to gain strength from the chaos of the past. Lovers have seven lifetimes to succeed. These two have already had six."

Her heart sank. Enguerrand was as stubborn as they came, and getting him to acknowledge his affection for Elara would be difficult. "Do I tell him?"

"That he and all those he's come to care about have less than seventy-two hours to live?" Hermes grimaced.

"Hermes, help me. Please." Tears burned her eyes. "I cannot lose my son."

His gaze dropped to their clasped hands, and his mouth firmed. Brelenia felt his fingers tighten, and his unimaginable power boosted hers.

"You won't, love. We'll do what we must."

He brushed away the single tear she shed. Balancing the drop on his finger, he shifted in Tripp's direction and blew, sending Brelenia's tear across the room to mingle with Elara's. Magic existed in the single drop.

"Courage, dear girl," he said. "Stand firm in your convictions this time." Shooting Brelenia a side glance, he grinned. "Perhaps you should invite her around for tea tomorrow, love. I have a plan to shake the ground under Tripp's feet."

"And not in an erupting volcano way?" she asked.

He laughed, snapped his fingers, and disappeared into a shimmering light.

The accusatory looks from her granddaughters hurt Florence. They'd been left alone to fend for themselves since they were teenagers. Yet, they weren't entirely alone. She'd always watched over them, instilling a magical tracker on their vehicles when they were out on dates, creating trusts for them to draw from after their parents disappeared, and chasing away anyone who didn't have their best interests at heart.

She glanced at Tripp.

He was the exception.

Although Flo suspected he truly cared about Elara, the man would ultimately break her girl's heart. Just as George Shaw had hers and Rupert Hawthorne had her daughter, Mae's. The Shaws were cursed in love. Had been from the beginning of time. All it took was one ancestor to run afoul of a jealous deity, and their family was marked for eternity.

Cutting a fleeting glance at the alcove, Flo grimaced. When Brelenia came to her with her cockamamie plan, Flo should've told her no. But the Goddess had promised she'd break the Shaw curse, stating if Flo didn't interfere between Tripp and Elara, things would be set to rights for their family.

"My entire line is to blame, Enguerrand," she told Tripp. Looking at her granddaughters, she tapped out a cigarette from its silver case and popped it in the corner of her mouth. Of course, she'd never light up inside the bookshop, but the comforting feel against her lip gave her courage in the face of their hostility.

Elara's wounded eyes were worse than Payton's frosty stare.

Flo shouldn't play favorites. Yet Payton, with her golden hair and narrow, upturned eyes, was the spitting image of her father, whereas Elara resembled Mae with her china-blue gaze and pale locks.

Wasn't she bound to be sentimental at her age?

"I still don't understand why you didn't say anything," Elara croaked as if holding back sobs. "We were so lost after… after… *so* lost."

"She's a mean bitch who doesn't care about anyone but herself," Payton stated coldly. She wrapped her arm around her sister's shoulders, and their unity was beautiful. "It probably never occurred to her to take us in. It might disrupt her hermit lifestyle."

"Florence doesn't deserve your scorn, Payton," Tripp said. "She's—"

"Don't." Flo shook her head. "You should go, Enguerrand. Restore time and take Dailey to the meeting. I'll be there soon."

As he began to object, the door blew open, and a swirl of snow accompanied a dark-haired man with piercing emerald eyes.

She whipped her head back toward the alcove. The man who had been with Brelenia was now the stranger at the shop entrance, brushing snow from his shoulders.

What the devil was going on?

He sent them a roguish grin. "The elements are in flux. Now I see why."

Tripp swore viciously and repeatedly, snagging everyone's notice and causing them to take a second glance at the newcomer.

"Elements?" Elara withdrew from Payton's comforting embrace and circled the end of the counter to peer out the window. "What in the forceful flurry is happening?" she exclaimed.

"It tends to happen when three witches from an ancient bloodline, a powerful warlock, and a demigod are in emotional turmoil." The dark-haired man frowned. "Although there isn't much coming from the exceedingly dull policeman. How is it possible?" he mused, almost to himself. "Tripp?"

"Those fucking boots."

"Ah."

Elara's focus ping-ponged between the two men. "You know each other?"

"Right. I forgot mortals these days aren't taught the old ways." The stranger held out his hand. "Hermes."

Slackjawed, she stared, earning a weary sigh from Tripp.

"My cousin," he said, glaring at Hermes. "What are you doing here?"

"I'd think it would be obvious. I've come to help you prevent a volcanic eruption."

CHAPTER THIRTEEN

Tripp Nightshade.

Elara shook her head.

He really was a demigod. Somehow, she'd convinced herself it wasn't true.

But he was related to Hermes, the man he'd labeled the Divine Trickster.

And Florence Shaw was her grandmother. One who couldn't be bothered to tell Payton or her the truth and barely paid them a living wage. If it wasn't for their trust funds—

The trust funds!

They were from their mother's mother, who, if Elara wasn't mistaken, was Flo. They'd never gotten that far into the conversation to find out. She assumed with the last name Shaw, Florence wasn't a Hawthorne, but she might've changed it for her own reasons.

Last night, she'd gotten through the rest of her shift on autopilot. Granted, it was shortened considerably when Flo told everyone to "get the hell out" and locked the doors behind them. Payton bolted immediately.

"I'm not waiting around to hear a pack of lies and excuses," she'd said as she grabbed her purse and stalked out the alley door.

Florence had appeared crushed but rallied in an instant. Chin in the air, she'd given Elara a do-your-worst look. But all the fight had left her, and the only thing she'd wanted at that moment was to leave Tripp, Flo, and Witchmere far, far behind. Her parents' nomadic lifestyle was looking better and better.

When Elara arrived home, she discovered Hex missing and spent the remainder of the night looking for him. Exhausted, depressed, and fearing the worst for her precious cat, she trudged back to her apartment and slept on the couch, jerking awake at every slight sound.

Snow fell outside the patio doors, and her worry for him doubled. Her pampered boy was never gone longer than a few hours, and he might not fare well in the harsh winter elements. Should she appeal to Tripp's better nature and ask him to alter the weather if he could?

Dismissing the idea, she considered others.

The Sandersons were wolf shifters. Their sense of smell should be more powerful than an average dog's, right? A quick internet search confirmed her guess. But which one did she approach? Katie? Bohdan? Certainly not Rowen. The brain-searing image of her hugging Tripp still rankled.

"Oh, Hex. Please come back to me," Elara said aloud, wishing with all her might that he was okay.

Less than two minutes later, a scratch at the glass doors caught her attention. With a cry of joy, she rushed to let Sir Hex-a-lot in. Sweeping him into her arms, she knelt on the floor and sobbed all over his snow-dampened fur.

"Where have you been?" she scolded between gasping breaths. "I thought... thought I'd l-lost you, Hex. You were... gone so l-long, and... and..." The stress of his disappearance, added to all she'd discovered the previous night, was too much, and her shuddering sobs wouldn't stop. Although Hex didn't struggle to get away, he didn't appear to love the torrential tearfest. "I l-love you... you stupid c-cat."

The expression on his face altered, and his emerald eyes grew softer as he stared at her.

"Meow." Hex's purr was deafening as he butted his head against her chin and rubbed his face along her jaw.

And then Tripp was there, shooing Hex from her arms and cradling her within his embrace. "Don't cry, flitter-mouse," he said in a low, aching voice as if her tears physically hurt him. "Please, don't cry."

Not questioning how he knew she needed comfort or why she accepted it when she wasn't happy with him, Elara climbed onto his lap, draped her arms around his shoulders, and buried her face against the strong column of his throat. The scent of his freshly showered skin was heavenly, and she sighed, feeling a strange contentment in being held.

Large, comforting hands rubbed circles on her back, and her eyes drifted shut as exhaustion washed over her. Remaining upset while secure in the arms of the man you adored was difficult, and her tears dried up.

"Why are you here?" she asked, pulling back to look at him.

"I was at *Wily Witches*, but you weren't. I also felt your angst, so I knew something was wrong." Tripp smoothed her hair, and his worried gaze traveled over her face. What he searched for, she couldn't say, but she assumed he wanted to make sure she wouldn't break down again before he released her.

His comment registered, and her jaw dropped.

"You *felt* my angst? Like literally felt it as a physical thing?"

He nodded and touched his chest. "Here. It's an ache."

Elara's gaze locked on the hand pressed to his heart, and hers melted along with her anger toward him. "How is it that you feel connected to me?"

"I don't know," he confessed. "It's been this way since I arrived in Witchmere and saw you."

She frowned, considering all the times she'd made an absolute fool of herself. Did he feel her discomfort or just her pain?

"When I... um, when I... was dodging you... I..." She swallowed, preparing to try again.

"Some," he said, taking pity on her. "Not as strong as the sensation has been since our first kiss."

What must it be like to have powers like his?

"Did you feel your other, uh, lovers' emotions?" She mentally kicked herself for asking when hesitancy crossed his face. "Never mind. It's okay."

"I don't have a problem answering, but I don't want to upset you further."

"Why would it upset me?"

"Because you don't believe my story about the boots, Elaina, and Élise."

"I do now," she confessed. "At least about the women. You can't live as long as you have without falling for someone, I imagine."

His gaze ate her up before settling on her mouth. "I keep telling myself I won't, but then I do."

"But you won't allow yourself to love fully? Why?"

Elara's question gave Tripp pause. Over the years, he'd told himself it was because gods and mortals didn't mix. If he were to sustain a severe wound, he'd heal. The likelihood of mortals doing the same was nil. But perhaps Elara was the exception. Her Shaw bloodlines produced extraordinary witches, though she'd yet to tap into her full magic. The Hawthorne side was rumored to be formidable, too, maybe more than the Shaws. However, his theory regarding her father's heritage was still a work in progress. Soon, Tripp would discover the truth.

Yes, the footwear was enchanted and the catalyst for her recent spells, but the abilities were all hers. Those blasted boots merely tapped into her considerable power, making both her and those damned things dangerous.

"Tripp?"

"Yeah, sorry. You threw me for a moment." He sighed and brushed a stubborn lock of hair from her brow. Whenever she tilted her head in inquiry, it tended to fall from its mooring behind her ear and obscure her soulful eyes.

"You don't have to answer," she hedged.

"I'm considering the question."

And he was.

Could his reticence be attributed to his mother's misguided matchmaking? His inability to settle down? The lack of desire to stay in one place longer than a decade?

Elara seemed to give up on a response and tucked her head in the crook of his neck. In the reflection of the patio door's glass, he saw her watching Hex, or rather, Hermes, as Tripp now knew the Trickster to be.

"That's not a regular cat, Elara. You'll need to come to terms with letting him go," he said gently.

"I love him."

Tripp's gut clenched. Yes, she believed Hermes was a dumb beast, but he knew differently. The knowledge of her caring for his cousin in any capacity tied his guts into knots.

"You don't truly know him."

The so-called cat locked eyes with Tripp, hiked up his leg, and began licking his balls.

"It looks like he winked at you," she said with a contagious giggle.

"He did," he replied sourly. "Let's make an appointment for him to get neutered tomorrow."

Hermes hissed and, with his tail puffed to three times its standard size, stalked from the room.

"Was it something I said?" Tripp asked dryly.

Straightening, Elara shifted her weight, preparing to abandon his lap. Unwilling to release her, he lifted her at the waist and resettled her to straddle him, putting them face to face. Her eyes flew wide, but she didn't object.

What he didn't expect was the feel of her heat against his dick, and the damned thing woke, ready to play.

Unable to keep his hands to himself, he wove his fingers into her thick hair, holding her head in place as he gazed deep into eyes that exposed her vulnerable soul.

He wanted to say, "Oh, flitter-mouse, you have no idea what you do to me." Yet the words stuck in the back of his throat, refusing to be uttered for fear of revealing his deepest desire.

Her.

When had she turned the tables and gained the upper hand? How had he become the flustered one, dodging encounters for self-preservation? Not to mention the preservation of others. Kissing her again could blow the lid off Rainier, and yet, he was tempted by forces stronger than him.

"What do you want from me, Tripp? Other than the boots."

Her solemn-voiced question struck to the heart of him.

"I don't know," he confessed hoarsely.

Her expression morphed into the carefully controlled one she presented to the world. The smile she offered was small and tight. Dismissive.

"Don't!" he barked, causing her to jump. Moderating his tone, he said, "Don't give me that look. Please. I hate it."

"What look?"

"The one that hides your true feelings. The one that says you don't need anyone because you're prepared to tough it out alone."

Surprise sent her jaw plunging, and Tripp couldn't ignore her siren's call another second longer.

"I'm going to kiss you, Elara Elizabeth Hawthorne, and if it's not what you want, say it now."

Heartbeats passed.

Finally, in answer, she dragged his head down and offered her mouth to him.

The moment their lips met, the world seemed to hold its breath, and then—like a dam breaking—raw, uncontainable energy surged between them. Elara clung to Tripp as the ground beneath their feet rumbled. Floor-tile cracks radiated outward like the earth was reacting to their union. In the distance, Rainier's snow-capped peak shivered. Its icy crown liquefied under the sheer heat of their connection, sending rivers of water cascading down its slopes. The kiss deepened into a storm of need and promise, and their power entwined until it was impossible to tell where his magic ended and hers began.

When they finally pulled apart, breathless and trembling, the air was thick with steam and power, the landscape forever marked by the fire they had unleashed.

A shadow blocked the morning's rays, and Tripp glanced up to find Hermes, naked-assed, staring out the patio doors toward the mountain.

"Fuck all, Tripp!" he snapped. "The villagers are going to want your head on a pike."

CHAPTER FOURTEEN

Elara's eyes flared wide, and she attempted to turn her head, but Tripp was faster and blocked her from viewing Hermes's perfect ass. He'd never had anyone compare his sculpted backside to his cousin's, but he wasn't taking any chances she might become enthralled by the sight.

"Is that Hermes?" she asked in a hushed voice. Her apartment wasn't exactly the size of the Taj Mahal, and the sound carried.

Hermes turned, giving them a full frontal, not in the least concerned about his nudity.

"Put that thing away, or it won't be the head above your shoulders on a pike," Tripp growled, continuing to block Elara's curious gaze.

With a gasp rivaling an outraged maiden, Hermes cupped himself. "What have I ever done to *you*?"

"Those fucking boots!"

"Yeah, well, those were originally intended for your mother and your deadbeat dad," he said with a dismissive shrug and snap of his fingers. Clothed in an outfit similar to the one he wore last night, he grinned. "You can release your woman. I've removed all temptation."

"Dick," Tripp retorted.

Hermes glanced down as if to check. "No. I've covered it."

Elara laughed, and Tripp was startled by the beautiful sound. Hermes, too. His attention locked onto her like a wolf does its prey.

"Don't even think about it," Tripp warned with a growl. "She's mine."

Satisfaction curled his cousin's lips, and color burst from the purple jewels on Elara's boots. She gasped and scrambled to her feet.

"Slow your roll, dude!" Her balled hands met her hips.

"What's the problem, flitter-mouse? You've wanted me since I arrived in this piddly little town."

Her dark scowl was worrisome. "Wait. You think you can come in here, demand I do what you want by giving up my cat and boots, kiss me so thoroughly it shakes the earth"—she pointed downward—"and cracks my tile, *then* have the nerve to *claim* me? Like I'm a fucking trophy you won as spoils of war? You also insulted my town. Are you cracked in the head?"

"Her tongue is sharp enough to castrate a man, isn't it?" Hermes crossed his arms and leaned against the wall, settling in for the entertainment. "I like this one, cousin."

"Fuck off already!" Tripp waved a hand and sent Hermes to the same lake Elara had dumped him after she received the boots. "Elara, flitter-mouse, listen—"

"No. I'm no pushover, Tripp Nightshade, so get that idea right out of your thick skull."

"I never said you were." He surged to his feet. "Hermes makes me and everyone else within a hundred-mile radius of him mad as a hatter. He delights in chaos, as I've warned you before. As a tool for his special brand of fuckery, those boots heighten your emotions. Which is precisely why I've been attempting to get them off you."

Her eyes narrowed. "Tell the truth. Was your intent to seduce me to give them up?"

The compulsion to tell the truth was too strong to resist. "Yes."

She paled. "You never wanted me before I put them on, did you?"

"I did want you, but I was never going to act on it."

A rush of blood flooded her face, turning her skin a fevered pink.

"The only reason you're doing it now is the boots, yes?"

"Yes."

Tears shimmered in her eyes, but she blinked them away and lifted her chin.

"And Hex? Who is he really?"

"Hermes."

The shock made her face slack, but crushing pain followed, contorting her features.

"Stay away from me, Tripp Nightshade. For now, forever."

The pull of an escape was strong. Despite the feeling of acid burning his skin, he fought the enchantment.

"Elara, listen to me," he demanded through gritted teeth. "Please, reverse your spell."

"There's no spell! It's a simple statement, and I don't ever want to se—"

Hermes clapped a dripping hand over her mouth. "Careful, love. As much as I hate to admit it, Tripp is correct. The boots amplify your emotions and use your natural abilities to create havoc."

She tugged his wrist until he released her. "Bullshit! I don't have that kind of magic."

"Look at his skin, Elara," he urged in a gentle tone one uses for wild animals. "Go on. He is physically hurting."

Her head whipped around just as Tripp held up his exposed forearms. Blisters were bubbling up and bursting, causing untold agony, all because he continued to fight her directive to leave.

"Tripp?" Her horror could bring tears to an onlooker's eyes. "How do I reverse it, Hermes? Tell me, please."

"Speak the words from your heart. The emotion you *truly* feel for him and not those caused by anger."

She rushed to Tripp, prepared to cup his face, but withdrew and clasped her hands over her heart. "I'm sorry. Your truth was hard to hear. In my rage, I wanted to send you away." Closing her eyes, she inhaled deeply. "Stay or go, Tripp. The decision is yours."

The heaviness in the air dissipated, and his wounds healed, leaving raw, angry marks in their place. It took longer for his face to stop burning. He expelled a relieved breath as the pain eased.

"I won't order you to go, but I will ask that you both leave me alone. Please," she said in a quiet voice. Her eyes were so large and tragic that it was impossible to refuse. Yet Tripp didn't want to abandon her in such a state.

"Elara—"

"Please, Tripp," she begged. "I need to be by myself for a while."

He met Hermes worried gaze over her head. When his cousin nodded, so did he. "All right. But will you have dinner with me tonight?"

"What's the point?" she asked tiredly as she sat down. With light fingers, she traced the jeweled pattern on the leather. "They are so beautiful and made me feel special."

He squatted and attempted to stroke her face, but she drew back, shunning his touch. With a regretful sigh, he said, "You *are* special, flitter-mouse. Unique and lovely, like no one else."

"I'm not. Not enough to make anyone stay." The single tear from her haunted eyes stung more than her unintentional spell.

"Elara," he whispered achingly. "The flaw isn't with you. It's with others."

Lifting her head, she locked gazes with him. "You're not flawed. You're perfect. So yes, the problem is me."

"No, I'm far from perfect. You're in love with this package." He waved a hand to indicate his body, then tapped his head. "Not what's in here."

"I've seen your many kindnesses when you think people aren't looking, Tripp. And you could buy from larger bookstores or online, but you support Flo's small business with your weekly orders."

"Those were so I could see you when I came by," he confessed.

She smiled, and the bittersweet quality killed him. "I always hid."

"I know, but not before I saw you."

The understanding that this might be the last time Elara looked upon his stunning visage caused an ache of such magnitude that she was sure her heart was breaking. The boots would need to be returned to Hermes, and she'd need to accept the truth that her beloved Hex was no more.

She shuddered as she recalled how the supposed cat hung out on the bed whenever she changed.

"Hermes, if you ever pose as a cat again, I'll find you and skin you alive," she warned.

He grinned, unrepentant. "At least I got to see you nude, and our boy Tripp never will."

The ground rumbled.

"I'm going to kill you, cousin," Tripp promised. "Mark my words."

Elara lifted her leg to remove the boot, but the zipper disappeared as she reached for the tab. Whipping her head up, she glared at Hermes.

"What's your game this time?"

"No game. The boots are charmed, and they don't feel their mission is completed."

"How does she get them off?" Tripp lurched to his feet, prepared for battle.

"She doesn't. Not until the two of you resolve your relationship."

"We just did," she said, jumping up and standing beside Tripp in unity.

He swung to stare down at her. "How so?"

She looked between him and Hermes, feeling like she was losing her mind. "I'm getting whiplash from all of this," she complained. "So okay, let me break it down for you. One: After what happened, we're on the same page and believe the boots gotta go."

"True."

"Two: Hex, aka Hermes, has to go."

"Agreed."

"Three: You don't want me like I do you—"

"Not true." Tripp wrapped his hand around her neck, tilting her head back to meet his intense gaze. "So not true, flittermouse. I've repeatedly told you, but you refuse to listen. Mortals and gods don't mix."

"So why not give up your powers?" Hermes suggested.

Tripp dropped his hand so fast Elara stumbled.

"It's a sacrifice I'm not willing to make for any woman," he ground out. "But she answered the objections you and your fucking boots might have, so remove them, Hermes."

"No can do, cousin!" He plopped down on the sofa and spread his arms wide along the top, grinning. "You have to resolve the love between you to the spell's satisfaction. You haven't."

"He doesn't love me," Elara told him.

Squinting one eye, Hermes crinkled his nose. "Doesn't he, though?"

"I'm never getting these damned things off," she cried in despair.

"Spill it, Hermes," Tripp ground out. "Now, before I tie your limbs like a fucking pretzel."

Weighing the threat, Hermes glanced between them. "I'll tell you, but only because I like Elara, and she has a rocking body I want to cuddle up with again."

Tripp lunged, diving into an empty couch.

From across the room, Hermes laughed. "You're so predictable."

Elara rose and pressed a hand to Tripp's chest, hoping to stop another charge.

What would a Trickster do in this situation if they wanted an answer? A wicked smile curled her mouth, and Hermes sobered.

"You'll tell us what you know, Divine Trickster, or I'll compel you to walk naked through Witchmere, clucking like a chicken."

"Sonofa—fine!" he snapped.

Tripp wrapped an arm around her shoulders and kissed her temple. "Nicely done, flitter-mouse."

Hermes resumed his place on the sofa, gesturing them to sit while he retold the tale.

CHAPTER FIFTEEN

Tripp was tangled up in knots after Hermes imparted his knowledge and left. "Fucking Hermes. And fucking Trickster bullshit."

"It's a lot to process," Elara replied.

"Your reincarnation and my idiocy?" Tripp rested his head against the back of the sofa as he stared morosely at the ceiling. How the hell had it come to this?

"Hermes said we must get it right because it's our last of seven chances. But what is considered *it*? Our relationship? We don't have one."

The ground rumbled, and Tripp recognized it as a reaction to his building irritation. Yet if he were honest with himself, he couldn't say she was wrong. They'd never taken the time to form anything resembling a connection. "We've had them in the past and seem to be dancing around one in the present. I think that counts."

"It's not like any I've experienced," she muttered, causing his annoyance to flare again.

"Now's not the time to bring in your past losers," he said, barely keeping his ire in check.

"Lovers."

"Whatever."

"Forget all that. What if we fuck it up?"

He snorted a laugh. Rarely did she swear, but her usage of the word "fuck" amused him.

"I don't think the problem is you, Elara."

"No, it's *us*. Together," she said. "And these stupid boots."

"I did try to warn you," he replied dryly.

"Oh, shut up."

Her grouchiness was funnier than her swearing, and Tripp bit the inside of his cheek to hold back his laughter. He rolled his head to the side and watched her animated visage as she worked through best-case scenarios.

"Do I go as far away from here as possible? Would that save Witchmere?" she asked.

"Wherever we go, disaster will follow." And the truth was depressing as hell.

"Not we. Me. With the boots." She shifted to face him, expression bordering on desperation. "I don't want you to get hurt any more than I want Payton and the rest of our town to suffer."

Giving in to his desire, Tripp stroked her petal-soft cheek. "I don't know the answer, flitter-mouse. But I suspect running will only make it worse at this juncture. The mountain will blow unless we find a way to combine our powers and those of a few others."

"These boots amplify my magic. That's a good thing, right?"

She appeared so hopeful, Tripp hated to crush her optimism, but he had no choice. "They do, but it's amplified in a bad way. Nothing good ever comes from Trickster enchantments."

"The question is, what will satisfy the spell?" She rose and poured them wine after offering him a drink. Returning, she handed off a glass and curled on the sofa beside him. "Lust, love, friendship?"

Sipping his wine, he considered the problem.

"I've offered all three over the years," he said. "Individually and together."

"Okay, so it needs something more. What haven't you ever given of yourself?"

Commitment.

The word burned into his brain as if branded by another. He opened his mouth to reply, then snapped it shut. There was no point in speaking up and rehashing the fact about gods and mortals mixing. Elara had heard it before and wasn't expecting anything from him.

He frowned.

She never had. Not in any lifetime before. Was her issue the lack of assumption? Did the Trickster *want* her to depend on Tripp? And how had her lack of faith in him altered his perception of what she wanted or needed in the past?

"What haven't you given of yourself in return?" he asked softly.

She appeared startled, as he had when she'd mentioned it. Shaking her head, she said, "How should I know? I don't remember any previous lifetimes. You're the one who finds me, according to Hermes."

Tripp sat straighter and shuffled through his memories.

"You're right. You moved to Witchmere first, and I gravitated toward this area. The same happened with Elaina, Élise, and the others."

"Okay, that's a clue, right?" Once again, her optimism surfaced. "There has to be a reason you find each incarnation of me."

"Maybe." But why? And more importantly, how? Was his attachment to her similar to a tracking device? "It makes me sound like a stalker," he muttered.

Elara grinned.

"I want to kiss you so badly," he confessed. "I'm going to lose man points by saying it, but I'm afraid if I do, it will cause a natural disaster."

Cupping his face, she brushed his nose with hers. "I get it. No kissing until we resolve the problem of the boots."

"Hermes sure knows how to torture a guy."

She laughed and released him to gather their glasses, but Tripp caught her wrist and drew her back down, settling her on his lap.

"I'm sorry you're caught up in this mess, Elara. If I could spare you and Witchmere, I would."

"It seems I'm a sucker for pretty shoes in every lifetime," she replied with a sigh. "It's not your fault, Tripp."

"No, it's not. I'm blaming Hermes and my mother for their inability to consider another's feelings or the lives of mortals."

"Don't. There's no point. We'll call a town meeting, tell everyone what's happening, and arrange for them to leave Witchmere."

"You heard my cousin. This half of the continent could be affected. We can't evacuate that many people in so short a time. Where would they go?" Tripp was sickened by the thought that so many would lose their lives. "I read a recent article about the bodies uncovered from the archeological dig around Mount Vesuvius. The pain and terror those poor fools must've suffered." He shook his head. "All due to those boots."

A shudder wracked Elara's body. "I'll admit, I'm terrified of fire and burning. I assumed I'd been burned as a witch in a previous life."

"I imagine those emotions are leftover from the London fire." He stroked her back. "I was beside myself with worry, but deep inside, I knew you'd perished."

"Do you think the trauma and pain caused you to hold back in our future relationships?"

Tripp paused the light caress. Had it? If so, it seemed reasonable enough. Why fully invest his heart only to have it broken again?

"You may be on to something, flitter-mouse."

"Why don't you speak with Harrison Cobb? He may have insight for you."

"He's likely to curse me than cure me after the Rowan incident."

Elara drew back. "'The Rowan incident?' Were you lovers?"

"No! You witnessed the hug."

"Oh." She rested her cheek against his chest. "Yes, well, the entire thing was fairly innocent, according to you. I'm sure Harrison will understand."

One look at Harrison Cobb's red face told Tripp the man didn't understand a damned thing. His new therapist was still enraged all these days later.

Tripp held up his hands. "She hugged me, Cobb. I've got a strong suspicion it was to make you jealous, seeing as it was right outside your window."

"And you happened to be there at that moment? The first available man she stumbled across and decided to use?"

"Yes."

"I don't believe you."

Tripp sighed. "It's true. I was stalking Elara."

Harrison's blond brows clashed.

"Not like that!" Tripp added hastily. "She knows."

Those expressive brows shot up.

"This, right here, is why I keep my own blasted counsel," he snapped.

"Then why are you here today?"

"It was Elara's idea. She seemed to think you could offer insight into my lack of commitment."

Harrison frowned. "Lack of commitment to her?"

"Yes."

"I'm afraid I'm confused. When she was here last week, she made it clear she avoided you at all costs. Not the other way around."

Tripp grinned. "Yes. She's a master at avoidance."

"I need context."

"Within thirty minutes of her departure, an earthquake shook Witchmere. Our kiss caused it."

"The earthquake?"

"Yes."

"I see." Harrison nodded thoughtfully as he watched him with considering eyes. "How often do you experience these delusions?"

"Excuse me?" Tripp stopped just shy of clearing out his ear with his finger. Surely, he'd misheard.

"This belief that you're capable of producing earthquakes by kissing a woman. How often do you—"

The earth rumbled as he jumped to his feet. "This is ridiculous!"

"Sit down, Mr. Nightshade," Harrison ordered. "I'm having a laugh at your expense."

"Not funny in the least, Cobb. Nor professional."

"True, but it was a little funny," the doctor replied with a smirk.

"Look, are you willing to help me or not? I have about forty-eight hours to figure this out."

"If you're causing the earthquakes, I suggest you stop kissing Elara." Harrison shrugged. "Problem averted."

"Except it's not just kissing that causes it," Tripp retorted.

"Well, don't do that either."

"I'm not... we're not... it's not..."

Again, the doctor smirked.

"More fucking shrink humor?" Tripp asked through gritted teeth.

"Yes."

"I'm done here." He rose, prepared to leave or level the building.

"I don't know why you're afraid to commit to her, Mr. Nightshade, but I suggest you examine your feelings about her and commitment." Harrison stood and set aside his notepad. "I'm serious on this point. You and I can discuss this at length, and if it saves Witchmere, I'm happy to devote all my time to finding the root cause. But you need to do the work, too."

"Where do I start?"

"How about the beginning?" Dr. Cobb was all business as he gestured to the sofa. "Have a seat and tell me about the first time you met her."

Tripp tried to recall the day, but Elara's visage was superimposed over Elaina's.

"Nightshade?"

"Yeah, sorry. I was thinking about Elara of today."

"How do the women differ?"

"She's stronger now, although less sure of herself around me. Then, she was vivacious and outgoing. About ten years younger and full of possibilities." Tripp closed his eyes as he envisioned Elaina. "But she was also less mature. She believed women were put on this earth for men to save them."

"Perhaps they were at that time."

"No. From the beginning, women have been the ones with the true strength. They birth babies, keep their family fed, and provide the love a man needs, all effortlessly." He grinned. "Women let men believe they're in charge, but a soft-spoken word and gentle touch make us putty in their hands."

"And you're putty in Elara's hands?"

Was he?

"I don't know. We haven't reached the soft-spoken word or gentle-touch stage. We've been at odds over those cursed boots."

"Cursed boots?"

"I should explain."

Ten minutes later, Harrison looked shell-shocked by the information Tripp imparted. "And she can't simply remove them? How does she sleep?"

"They come off at night but form a protective bubble so no one can touch them but her. Every morning, she's compelled to put them back on."

The doctor's expression turned outraged. "Trickster magic is taking away her agency?"

"Yes and no. Yes, in that she's forced to see this enchantment through. No, because she's ultimately in charge of her fate. And all of ours." Tripp rested his elbows on his knees as he considered how to explain. "Your brother was unkind to Payton, and Elara sent him running away with his tail between his legs. She's powerful. More than anyone in this town while she's wearing those things."

"But if they are compelling her to be mean—"

"They aren't. Her life experiences are bubbling up, and she's not taking any prisoners."

Harrison appeared concerned. "Tripp, I can't betray her confidence, but she has a lot of issues from this lifetime alone. Add in her experiences from the previous ones, and you may have a ticking time bomb on your hands."

"That's what I've been trying to tell you. We have about forty-eight hours to resolve this mess. What am I missing?"

"What haven't you given to her?"

The question caused Tripp to jerk upright. "She asked the same thing."

"She's clever. I'd be surprised if she hadn't." Harrison tilted his head. "What did you say?"

"Nothing. I turned the question on her."

"What did she say?"

"She said she doesn't remember and that I was the one who always found her," Tripp said.

"And is she correct?"

"Yes. I'm a fucking moth to her flame, but I'm not sure why. What power does she hold that no other woman does?"

Harrison laughed. "If you figure that one out, I want to be the first to know."

CHAPTER SIXTEEN

Tripp Nightshade.

If Elara didn't work with him and find a way to appease the Trickster, he and all the lovely residents of Witchmere would die. She couldn't bear the idea of his beautiful light extinguished.

Leaning on the balcony railing, she observed the bustling street below with detachment. What good did it do to care? Christmas was less than four days away, and their town, with its holiday tourists, might never live to see it—all because of *her*.

She closed her eyes and said, "Come to me, Hex, er, Hermes."

When she lifted her lids, she was startled to see him standing before her. Those green eyes were more penetrating as a human, and his ire at being summoned was stronger than any irritation Hex had displayed. This time, he couldn't hike a leg and lick his balls to show annoyance.

Elara almost laughed at the mental image.

"What do you want?"

"Maybe I miss my cat," she replied with a chin lift.

His eyes raked her body. "I wouldn't mind curling up with you again."

"Pervert." But if she weren't crazy about Tripp, she'd be all over him like a hobo on a ham sandwich.

Hermes's grin was too knowing for her peace of mind.

"So, can I throw myself into the volcano to pacify the Gods, or what?" she asked, wiping the amusement from his face.

"Elara."

Tears stung her eyes. "Please, Hermes. Tell me what I can do to save my friends and family. I'll do anything."

"It isn't as simple as that, love."

Turning away, she watched the unsuspecting go about their business. "I'll stay and clean up my mess, but can you implant a suggestion for everyone to leave?"

"It would be a mass exodus, and people might get hurt, considering the scope of the situation."

"It's not like they're going to live anyway, right?" Angry, she stalked inside.

"Elara." His tone was understanding and irritating.

"Just go away, Hermes. You're useless."

"Careful."

The warning note in his voice sent her into a rage. "Why? What's the worst you can do? Curse me with magical boots that will kill hundreds of thousands of innocents because Tripp and I can't figure out what the fuck you want from us?" She charged over and shoved his chest, spiking her fury because he didn't budge.

"Fuck you, Hermes, and the horse you rode in on! Or is it a Pegasus? I don't even know your stupid Greek God history."

The ground rumbled, halting her next rant.

They both froze, eyes wide.

"Did I do that?" she croaked.

"I don't know." He recovered quicker than her. "But how about you keep your anger to a minimum?"

"Good plan." With shaking hands, she pushed back her hair. "I can do that."

"I explained earlier that you and Tripp need to resolve your relationship. It may mean you set aside your doubts and come together in love, or it could mean you find common ground and walk away from each other forever. The answer isn't cut and dry, Elara. It never is."

"We have less than two days, and we've never had the chance to explore a relationship. It's not fair to expect it of us, Hermes."

"You've danced around each other for two and a half years, not counting the many lives before this one."

She threw up her hands. "I don't remember any of them!"

"No, but Tripp does. He also knows someone who can restore your memories if he cares to ask."

"Who?"

"My father."

"Zeus?" she screeched.

"I see you *do* know your Greek God history," he replied dryly.

"Yeah, well, I learned enough to know asking a god for anything will cost more in the long run."

"Sometimes, yes." Hermes strolled over to her bookshelves and nudged the snow globe her father had given her as a child. It inched precariously close to the edge.

"Your inner cat must be itching to get out," she said, removing temptation from his path. After setting the snow globe on the bottom shelf, she straightened and met his laughing gaze squarely. "What do you think Zeus would demand as payment from Tripp? I assume a mortal like myself would be beneath his notice."

"Clever girl."

"I've had to be. Answer the question."

Hermes shrugged and explored the shelves she'd refused to let Hex climb. "Firstborn? I'm not privy to my father's thoughts nor inclined to care."

"Firstborn? As in *child?*" Elara shook her head vehemently. "Not a chance! No way am I allowing Tripp to sacrifice his child on my behalf."

"He might not have one if you don't." Hermes acted like he didn't care one way or the other.

"What the hell is that supposed to mean?"

"It means we'll both be dead by then, flitter-mouse," Tripp said from behind her.

She whirled to face him. "Why aren't you furious at this ridiculous suggestion?"

"Because I have no intention of asking my uncle for anything." Striding forward, he cupped her jaw. "We'll figure it out, or we won't. But this is our problem to work through."

"I did this, Tripp. You warned me to remove the boots, and I didn't listen."

He opened his mouth to reply, but Hermes inserted a hand between them.

"If I may... You couldn't have resisted even had you wanted to, Elara. They are enchanted."

Balling her hands into fists, she rounded on him. "So this setup is centuries old? We were always going to be screwed?"

"Not necessarily. At any time, you could've given in to your love for each other and—"

"That's it!" The first stirring of excitement bubbled within her. "It's never been about resolving any issues or walking away. You won't be happy without a commitment."

Satisfaction curled his mouth. "Like I said, clever girl."

On the heels of her epiphany rode the cold, hard truth. There was no way she or Tripp could fool the boots by the deadline. They weren't in love.

"Mount Rainier will blow," she stated with finality. "We need more time."

Hermes glanced at Tripp, then back at her. "I'll leave you to talk this through."

Elara's tragic expression was a gut punch. Tripp's desire to haul her into his arms was overwhelming, but giving in to the urge was useless. They knew the score.

"What are you doing back here? I thought you had an appointment with Harrison?" she asked dully.

"Your distress distracted me."

"I'm sorry. I should've—"

Expelling a heavy sigh, he gave in to the desire and drew her close. "Stop apologizing, flitter-mouse. I'd rather be here."

Her "You're just saying that" was muffled and barely audible against his chest.

"No. If these are to be our last hours, I want to spend them with you." He smiled when her arms tightened around him.

"Would more time have helped us fall in love, do you think?" she asked.

Her wistful question caused his heart to ache. "Doubtful. I won't say love is instantaneous, but either you love someone, or you don't. Trying to build what isn't there won't work."

"And you don't love me," Elara stated flatly.

"The attraction is present," he countered. "I like you more than anyone I've met while living here."

She processed his comment, then nodded. "You've found me every lifetime, according to you and Hermes. But we can't get to the love part because someone is always delivering me a pair of cursed shoes, starting the clock."

The idea that they were being sabotaged never crossed his mind before she oh-so-innocently voiced it. If an outside interference was disrupting the Fates' design, could he appeal to a higher power to sort it out? Would they give him the required time or magic to prevent Rainier's explosion? It bore looking into.

A phone on the counter heralded an incoming text, and Elara released him to check the message.

"Anything important?" Tripp asked, sensing her unease.

"There's been a town meeting called at *Wily Witches*. You and I are being ordered to attend."

"Ordered? Who would dare?"

"According to Payton, your mother dared."

Holding back the litany of swear words struggling to escape, he nodded. "Do you wish to walk or teleport?"

Her eyes rounded. "I've never... I mean, I want to, but... My magic, it's..."

"Elara."

She pressed her fingertips to her mouth and waited.

"If you'd like to try it, I'm happy to transport you wherever you wish," he assured her.

"Truly?"

He smiled at her childlike wonder. "Truly."

"What do I do?"

"You hold on to me until I tell you to let go," he replied.

A wry smile curled her lips. "I think I can do that."

Tripp sensed her meaning was far, far deeper, but he ignored it. Standing, he drew her to her feet and into his arms. "Ready?"

"Mmhmm."

"Take a deep breath and clear your mind. When we arrive, you may feel discombobulated or dizzy. It's normal for the first time."

"Okay."

In his mind's eye, he envisioned the alleyway beside the coffeehouse. Long ago, the alleys of Witchmere were enchanted, allowing for quick travel without revealing the supernatural. If non-magical pedestrians were about, they wouldn't see the instantaneous comings and goings of the residents.

"You can open your eyes now, flitter-mouse."

Tripp was unprepared for the impact when she did. The lazy way she lifted her lids and the unsuppressed excitement glowing from those blue orbs packed a powerful punch, making it difficult to look away. His desire to kiss her was overriding his ability to think straight.

"None of that," his mother called from the alley entrance. "We've important matters to attend, darling."

He briefly considered stealing Elara away to an undisclosed location to spend time alone with her. They'd yet to experience a day of peace and quiet or simply exist in the moment. All the external factors were pushing them farther apart rather than allowing them to bond, and Tripp couldn't help feeling it was the opposite of what they were meant to experience.

Facing her, Tripp grimaced. "None of that? Wasn't your whole goal to find me a mate, Mother?"

"Don't be cheeky, darling. That mountain is about to erupt, and I'd prefer not to have another disaster on my hands."

"Then stop sending lethal boots to women I care about," he snapped.

Her smile flashed, quickly replaced by compressed lips and a narrow-eyed look. "Take a deep look at your feelings, and soon," she urged. Wiggling her fingers at Elara as if encouraging a child to take her hand, Brelenia said, "Come, my dear. We have things to discuss."

Ever dutiful, Elara took her proffered hand, leaving him standing, frustrated and all alone.

"Story of my life," he muttered.

The mountain rumbled in response.

CHAPTER SEVENTEEN

Tripp Nightshade.

Seeing him spearhead the discussion to save Witchmere was eye-opening for Elara. Previously, she'd viewed him as something of a player, but if she'd bothered to consider anything other than those glorious shoulders, she'd be forced to admit there was much to admire about him. His many kindnesses to the townspeople of Witchmere were primary. Tripp never failed to wish someone a good morning or flash a genuine smile at the elderly residents as they passed. He held open doors and carried packages, too. Never once had he failed to resolve a conflict if he stumbled across one.

Tripp Nightshade was a born peacemaker and leader.

"And he'd make a helluva lot better mayor than that cow, Mary-Alice Cobb," Elara muttered.

"What was that, dear?" Brelenia asked, leaning forward. "Did you say something about a cow?"

Casting a panicked glance at the Mayor, Elara shook her head. "I'm sure you misheard, ma'am."

"Hmm. Possible, but doubtful," she said.

They'd been formally introduced thirty minutes ago, and Elara couldn't help but like the woman. Although Tripp's mother was a goddess, she was down-to-earth and kind, like him. Granted, the salty feelings hadn't disappeared, and Elara didn't love another person determining her fate. Yet a fifteen-minute explanation from Brelenia told her all she needed to know. Beside her was a caring mother, regardless of the fact that she was a deity, and she only wanted the best for her son. Indeed, *all* her children.

How could Elara fault her for interfering? Especially now, the Goddess was involving herself in rectifying the situation and mitigating the damage caused by the boots.

But would their efforts be in vain?

She glanced at Hermes, surprised to find him watching her. The standard mischievous gleam in his eyes was missing, and there was a disturbing seriousness in its place.

"What?" she mouthed.

Humor caused the outer corners of his eyes to crinkle and his mouth to twitch as he fought a smile.

"Do you two have something to share with the rest of the class?" Payton asked with an arched brow.

Elara elbowed her into silence and sent an apologetic grimace Tripp's way when he paused.

His wink allowed her to relax.

Never had she feared him in the past, but he was a demigod, and the Gods were fickle creatures. Sitting straighter, she realized she'd just put her finger on why she found it difficult to commit—and possibly why it was impossible for him to. She didn't trust him to treasure her heart for the long run. But were his reasons reversed? Did he fear outliving her and suffering a broken heart due to his immortality? How awful to live longer than everyone else and continuously suffer loss.

Tingling started in her toes, spreading along the soles of her feet and sending warmth up her legs. Her breathing ratcheted up, becoming erratic as the heat within turned unbearable.

"Elara!"

Tripp practically demolished the coffeehouse's private room as he shoved tables and chairs out of his way to get to her. Anyone with an ounce of self-preservation jumped up and cleared the path. The room turned into a kaleidoscope of color and sound, with all the shapes spinning out of control and conversations running together.

"I don't feel well," she confessed as he reached her. Raising a shaky hand to her forehead, she gasped when she touched her scalding skin. "Tripp?"

"Stay calm, flitter-mouse," he urged, but the panicked look he sent his mother was at direct odds with his calm tone.

"Tell her, Florence," Brelenia said. "Your granddaughters need to understand who and what they are."

"What are we?" Elara gasped, not truly caring, as she searched for a water pitcher or anything cold to cool her burning body. Light flared inside an empty glass, and within the blink of an eye, the vessel was filled to the brim with ice water.

"Did I do that?" she croaked.

"Yes." Florence circled the table, her expression troubled. "I thought I had more time, but listen to me, gel. The Hawthorne line—"

"No!" Mayor Cobb leaped up and slapped her palm on the table. "They're not prepared for the knowledge—or the gift."

"Well, it's happening either way, isn't it?" her grandmother snapped. "True power comes from embracing her vulnerabilities and strengths, which is clearly what she just did if her body's transitioning."

"Transitioning?" Elara squeaked. "What am I transitioning to?"

"A Titan."

Payton fumbled the glass she was offering Elara. After righting it, she glared at Florence. "A *what?*"

"Titan," Brelenia supplied with a sympathetic glance at Tripp. "I'm sorry, darling."

Frowning darkly, he shook his head. "Don't be. She needed to know."

"Wait, what?" Feeling as if the meat of her body was cooking and peeling off the bone, Elara gasped and guzzled the water

Payton had given her. With a pant, she gestured for the pitcher. "Tripp? You knew and withheld this information?"

Rainier rumbled.

"Elara, stay calm and listen carefully," he urged.

"This is as calm as I get," she snapped. "Somebody better start talking before I spontaneously combust and take that fucking mountain top with me."

"You are the three-time great-granddaughter of Helios," Florence explained, waving and refilling Elara's glass. "Our line is ancient, as old as Brelenia's, and just as powerful."

"Who the hell is Helios?" Groaning, Elara emptied her third glass. "And why the hell didn't I pay attention in school?"

"I'm not sure they taught things like Greek mythology where we ended up," Payton replied.

"How would you know? You quit your sophomore year."

"Elara!" Florence scolded, appearing disappointed in her retort.

Yet, along with the burning cells came a snarky attitude Elara couldn't suppress. As her body flooded with magic, her mind twisted, and her heart hardened. Only a tiny part of her regretted her comeback, but she felt as if her compassion were being snuffed out.

"Why now? Why is this taking over my body, and how do I stop it?" she demanded, downing another glass.

"You don't," Brelenia said. "And the influx of emotions, good and bad, is normal. Don't try to fight the transformation."

Payton, ever Elara's staunch supporter, grew enraged. "You knew about this and sent those fucking boots anyway? We'll all be lucky if the mountain doesn't take out half of the States in my sister's condition."

"That's why it's imperative she remain calm," Tripp said, refilling Elara's water as soon as she finished it. "And hydrated."

"Why am I craving this much water? The heat?" she asked.

"Partially. I believe the other reason is your water nymph heritage."

"What? As in *mermaid?*"

Elara looked at Tripp in disbelief, and he didn't blame her one bit. To find out one was descended from the Sun God, Helios, and was technically a mashup of Titan and water nymph would be a lot for anyone to process.

"Yes, as in mermaid, but without the tail."

"This is a joke, right?" Payton pushed him out of the way and placed a palm against Elara's flushed forehead. As soon as her sister winced and hissed, she dropped her arm and wrung her hands together. "She's burning up. Let's get her to the hospital. This fever can't be normal."

Tripp snorted. "Nothing about this situation is normal. But a hospital will do her no good. She's mid-transformation."

"Yeah, but what am I transforming into?" Elara asked. "You said no tail, but will I grow into a seven-foot monster with horns and cloven feet? Because it feels like the fires of Hell inside my skin."

"Mother? Florence? Care to field this one?"

Neither of them had an answer and merely shrugged.

"Way to put her mind at ease," Payton snapped.

Rainier rumbled, and he poured Elara another glass of water. "Careful, flitter-mouse. Yes, you're flushed, but your physical appearance hasn't changed, and it's doubtful it will. This transformation is internal, which is why it feels like your insides are on fire."

"When will it be over?" she asked.

"I've never seen another go through this, so I can't say." He glanced at Florence, who was suspiciously tight-lipped about her granddaughter's dilemma. The longer it went on, the angrier at her he became. The Hawthorne girls should've been informed of their heritage when they were old enough to decide if they wanted their powers bound or risk turning.

Elara's back arched, and her head dropped backward. A

column of pure white light flew skyward from her gaping mouth, and her blue eyes iced over.

Panicked, Tripp turned to the one person likely to give him answers.

"Hermes? Is this normal?" Elara's spontaneous combustion worry seemed more probable by the minute. And the damnable part of it was not his fear for others so much as he feared for her. Bearing witness to her pain but being helpless to ease her discomfort was killing him. "Please tell me what you know."

"Not much more than you do," Hermes admitted with a distasteful twist of his lips. "I'm sorry, Tripp. I wish I did."

"Is everyone here saying they've never encountered a descendant of the Titans? What about you, Florence? This is your fucking granddaughter!"

"She's never cared about anyone but herself." Payton's look was sullen, bordering on sad. Her neglect by parents and grandparents alike was written on every line of her unhappy face.

"Will your father help, Hermes?" Tripp asked, willing to sacrifice whatever he had to if it ensured Elara's wellbeing.

"You don't need my brother," Brelenia said, shifting him out of the way to approach her. "Trust the process, Enguerrand. If she's worthy, she'll survive."

"What?" His incredulous tone matched Payton's as they hollered the word together.

"If the Gods deem her worthy, she'll survive the transition," his mother repeated calmly. Yet there was a tightness in the lines around her mouth and eyes.

"And if they don't, everyone in Witchmere is doomed," Mayor Cobb stated grimly. In fairness, she was always grim, but her comment was especially dire.

Dailey and Payton exchanged a look, and Tripp experienced a sympathetic pang for them.

Archer Roche rose to his feet. "I've witnessed the transition. Elara will come out stronger on the other side of it."

"How long does this go on?" he asked. "What can we do to ease her suffering?"

"Not much longer. A day at the most. And nothing. It's a test of the Gods, and she must endure to be worthy."

Unable to bear another second of watching her convulse, Tripp gathered Elara close, careful to avoid the searing light. He'd offer her any comfort he could while she was withstanding the pain.

"I'm here, flitter-mouse. I'm here," he whispered. "I'll not let you go."

With one last buck of her body, the light snuffed out, and she sagged within the circle of his arms. The boots fired up, and colorful beams exploded from the jewels. Beneath them, the ground woke, no doubt sending Richter-scale alerts across the country with the quake's magnitude. Those attending the meeting looked wary.

"Is she causing this?" Payton asked. Fear caused her voice to tremble, but she lifted her chin as if she would take on the fire gods to save her sister.

"I don't know," he admitted. "It may very well be me."

What he felt couldn't be called love, but Tripp cared a whole helluva lot. And he certainly didn't want to live in a world without Elara to brighten his days. If it came down to it and his destiny was to do so, he'd place himself directly on Rainier's lip when she blew.

CHAPTER EIGHTEEN

"Should we continue without them?" Brelenia asked, her eyes following her son's departure. In his arms, he cradled Elara, and his worried expression spoke well for the resolution of their magical boots experience.

"What's the point?" Mayor Cobb gathered her pad, pen, and purse. "Without the two primary instigators of this catastrophe, we're dead in the water."

Brelenia narrowed her gaze. "I don't believe I care for your tone, Mary-Alice."

"I know I don't," Payton added. With hands on her hips and the light of battle in her eyes, she stared the mayor down. "How about you try to be a human being and consider other people's feelings for a change, you miserable heifer?"

"How *dare* you!" Mary-Alice's outrage was complete.

Brelenia shared an exasperated glance with Florence before clapping her hands. "Enough, ladies. Fighting amongst ourselves will solve nothing."

Dailey Cobb showed a marked interest in the fireworks between his mother and Payton, and it forced one to wonder if he remained on the sidelines for fear of backlash from both women or if he wanted them to work through their issues on their own.

Brelenia could've told him it wasn't going to happen. Mary-Alice might be a loving mother under her polished exterior, but in her mind, Payton Hawthorne wasn't good enough for her precious boy. Having been in a similar situation with her middle child, Brelenia understood that letting her son make his own mistakes was paramount. Perhaps, when Rainier was put to rest, she'd pull the other woman aside to suggest she exit Dailey and Payton's relationship. Maybe then the couple might stand a chance.

Peering closer, she spotted the magic she'd previously missed. The air around him was tinged purple, giving Brelenia a strong indication Elara had either purposefully or accidentally cast a spell on Dailey. One that might be difficult to remove since it was enhanced with Trickster magic. It was a wonder that Enguerrand and Hermes had failed to notice it. Granted, they might have, but they had yet to act. Certainly, Enguerrand was preoccupied with Elara. Hermes, as the God of Chaos, may have ignored the spell in favor of the upcoming drama. One never knew with her mischievous nephew.

Filing the information away for another time, Brelenia focused on the unfolding discussion.

"This is everyone's problem," Florence was saying. "Why can't you get it through that helmet-haired head of yours, Mary-Alice?" She flipped open her cigarette case, eyed the Mayor's hairspray-coated up-do, and snapped the lid closed with a huff. "Might cause an explosion well before Rainier blows her top."

Brelenia bit the inside of her cheek to hold back her laughter. She dared not meet Hermes's gaze, or she'd lose control. If he displayed any humor whatsoever, she was what her son called "a goner."

"Are you going to sit there and let them talk to me like this, Dailey James?" Mary-Alice asked frostily.

Dailey dropped his booted feet from the table and stood. "No, ma'am. That wasn't my intent. But you've never needed me to defend your honor in the past. When you're all ready to discuss the problem, call me. I've rounds to make."

"Let another of your officers do it," she ordered. "You're needed here."

Indecision was written on his face, and he scratched his jaw with its day-old stubble. "I need a coffee," he muttered, striding from the room toward the barista.

"Another one bites the dust," Payton quipped. "Soon, we won't have anyone in attendance, Mayor. Keep up the charming dialogue."

"And yet, the only one not contributing anything to this discussion is *you*, dear," Mary-Alice replied with a chilly smile.

If hatred had a look, it was in the one Payton Hawthorne cast her ex-lover's mother.

Hermes jumped up, casually gripped her arm, wrapped it through his, and escorted her toward the exit. "Come, you beautiful creature. Tell me more about your charming town."

Although he'd defused the bomb, his departure with Payton sparked another fuse.

"That is precisely why she's no match for my son!" Mary-Alice sneered. "She runs off with other men at every opportunity. She's nothing but a who—"

"Careful," Florence warned. "That's my kin you're disparaging, and I'll not stand for it."

"You're the reason they are as wild and unpredictable as they are, Florence Shaw. If you'd revealed what they were and sent them to be trained in a proper academy, we might not be in this dire circumstance."

"Sure, and it's always my fault, isn't it, you harpy! Maybe if you hadn't been throwing yourself at Rupert, my Mae might've stuck around."

"How *dare* you!" Mary-Alice exclaimed.

"Oh, get off your high horse, you mad cow! Own up to your mistakes for once."

Archer Roche sighed and exited the room, leaving Brelenia, the two lifelong foes, and Bohdan Sanderson lurking in the shadows.

"Mr. Sanderson, would you be so kind as to fetch a pot of tea while I speak to these ladies?" she asked, casting her most encouraging smile. "You'd be a dear if you would."

Humor brightened his sharp gaze, and he strode away. Before exiting, he turned back and ascertained her favorite before continuing his mission.

The instant he was gone, Brelenia flicked a finger to shut the door behind him, then turned to face the bickering town leaders. She tapped her fingernail against her teeth as she considered her options. Sure, she could freeze and force them to behave, but it would solve nothing. They needed to work together for the good of the community and, eventually, Payton and Dailey.

"Ladies," she called, hoping to gain their attention. She failed. With an irritated sigh, she shut her eyes and summoned her ability to influence others. When she had a handle on the power, she considered the words to convey what she intended and wove them into her short speech. "You will shelve this unnecessary argument until the threat has passed and Witchmere is once again safe, do you understand?"

They nodded, and the battle line was erased as they joined her at the table.

Bohdan returned with the tea, followed by Archer, Hermes, and Payton.

"Perfect timing, everyone." Brelenia's smile was warm and welcoming, including them all. The more people she could rally to work together, the better the potential outcome. "Where is Officer Cobb? Will he be rejoining us?"

"Dailey is making the rounds. He'll be back in ten," Archer informed them.

Interesting. Despite his mother's dictate to assign the job elsewhere, Dailey had defied her. Progress, indeed. The young man wasn't what one would call a "mama's boy," but coming from a tight-knit magical family as he had, he was inclined to listen to the matriarch. Payton, on the other hand, was left to find her way in the world without proper guidance. Both possessed strong personalities, but where Dailey's life was structured, Payton's wasn't, and the woman would always rebel whenever anyone attempted to control her.

"Let's get started—again—shall we?" Brelenia suggested sweetly.

Hermes grinned at her masterful manipulation but remained silent.

"The problem is that Enguerrand and Elara can't acknowledge their feelings for each other. I propose we put operation *Jealousy* into motion."

With green eyes sparkling, Hermes leaned forward. "That's Tripp's given name, for those who don't know." Of Brelenia, he asked, "How do you propose we do that? Which of the townspeople do you intend to utilize for your plan?"

"The clear choice is Rowan Sanderson to entice Tripp," Florence suggested. "She's the most beautiful gel in town."

All the men nodded.

Payton scowled but held back her opinion.

"Excellent." Brelenia poured tea into the available cups and passed them out. "And who should we use to open my son's eyes? Hmm?"

"I doubt you'll have any takers. Who the hell is going to risk a demigod's temper?" Archer asked dryly.

She nodded. "Yes, I can see where that might be a problem." Focusing her attention on Hermes, she raised a brow. "I suppose you'll have to volunteer, nephew."

"No can do." He shook his head, considered the tea in the delicate cup, and waved a hand to transform it into a glass of wine.

"You'd best make sure you turn that back. Avery will have your ass if all her cups and saucers aren't accounted for," Bohdan warned.

"Duly noted," Hermes replied.

"Back to the discussion. Why can't you volunteer?" Payton asked him.

"She knows who I am and that I posed as her beloved cat. Her tolerance for my presence is low."

"Valid." She cast a glance among those present, summing them up. "Bohdan might be her type. He likes to lurk in alleyways."

The man in question choked. When he could speak again, he said, "Hell, no! Tripp threatened to have my ass waxed the last time I annoyed him. I'm not going anywhere near Elara."

Unable to escape the visual of a bald-assed wolf, Brelenia laughed along with the others. "Archer? What about you? Would you be willing to court Elara to prompt Enguerrand to react?"

He appeared to consider it but quickly shrugged and shook his head. "I wouldn't pass as handsome with today's women. I doubt Tripp would view me as a threat to his relationship, given how enamored Elara is with him. Honestly, I doubt he'd view anyone that way."

"You have a point. He takes after me and is gifted in the looks department." She wasn't intentionally vain. The truth was that the Gods were a gorgeous lot. Although plastic surgery, eating nutritious foods, and exercise could make mortals beautiful, few reached her level. She might be older than dirt, but she still possessed the ass of a twenty-year-old.

"My suggestion would be to bring out his protective instincts," Hermes said. "Perhaps another god or Titan might work to spark his territorial side."

Brelenia tapped a manicured finger on the table as she considered the problem from every angle. Her lips curled as she met and held her nephew's emerald gaze. He turned wary, amusing her further.

"An abduction," she declared. "Tomorrow. And I know just the person to do it."

CHAPTER NINETEEN

"You should know, your mother has planned to spark your protective instincts where your woman is concerned," Hermes told Tripp an hour later.

Pausing in bathing Elara's brow, Tripp scowled. "What? Why?"

"She's hoping, if you're challenged, you'll realize the depths to which you care for Elara."

He hung his head and sighed. "Go ahead. Tell me everything. What does she intend to do?"

"Abduction. I know the when—tomorrow—but not the who. She seemed to have another deity in mind, though."

"Fucking lovely."

In truth, it wasn't the first batshit crazy idea his mother had, but it might be the most dangerous. Elara had yet to wake from her transformation, if it was indeed over, and his concern was at an all-time high. She'd been fighting a fever since the meeting, and Tripp had done his level best to cool her skin with ice water. Most of the moisture had turned to steam.

He was still wrapping his mind around the level of magic radiating through and off her.

"It's possible she's stronger than we are," he said aloud.

"Your mother?" Hermes asked, confusion tugging his brows down.

"Elara. Focus on her power and see for yourself."

Shutting his eyes, his cousin remained still as he tested the air between them. When his emerald eyes flared wide, he confirmed what Tripp suspected.

"How can that be?" Hermes asked.

"Well, now we know Helios sired her line. He's a formidable god." With gentle fingers, he spread water along the seam of her parched lips. "I'm worried about her," he confessed. "It's as if something is sucking all the fluid from her body, and her skin is dehydrating faster than I can replenish it."

"What about a humectant applied to her skin? Would it help?"

"I've tried it on her face. It dried instantly, creating a puff of dust." Tripp shook his head. "Don't ask me how it happened because I don't know."

"We need to speak to Florence Shaw."

"It may not do any good," he replied. "Although she's a formidable witch in her own right, with the nymph blood running through her veins, she's not a Titan-nymph hybrid like Elara."

"But surely she possesses an inkling of how it works," Hermes argued.

"One would think, but I received the impression earlier that she didn't. I've known her for a few years, and she's never been shy about information or opinions."

"Have you tried adding salt to the water?" his cousin asked, shrugging when Tripp paused in bathing Elara's skin. "If she's part water nymph, she needs the sea."

"You're a brilliant bastard, I'll grant you that." Gathering her close, Tripp envisioned the closest beach, but as he was about to teleport, Hermes touched his arm.

"Wait. I have a different idea. We should take her to Storm Bringer's Bay."

"Are you mad?" Tripp shook his head. "The Storm Bringer will require a token, and we have nothing to give."

"She owes me a favor."

Storm Bringer's Bay was by far the best option. Secluded and magical, the waters were reported to heal a weary traveler. But the water nymph who'd claimed the bay for her own was notoriously demanding. Unless at their wits' end, deities stayed far away from Storm's seductive waters lest they found themselves indebted to an exacting nymph.

"How is it *she* owes *you*?"

"I helped her exact the price from a would-be thief."

Glancing down at Elara, Tripp turned it over in his mind and considered all his options. Even as he delayed, her lips cracked and dried. Blood oozed from the worst cracks.

"All right. Take me to her."

They were standing at the water's edge in a flash, facing the Storm Bringer.

"Storm! Darling!" Hermes called with a roguish grin. "I've come to call in that favor."

Dark skin glistening with water, the naked nymph rose from the water to stand on its surface. With eyes narrowed, she sashayed to them, creating the barest of ripples. "You dare come here, Hermes?"

"Fuck," Tripp muttered under his breath. "I should've known."

Leave it to the Divine Trickster to con him into going where they weren't welcomed and where the toll was likely the cost of their lives.

"I've got this," Hermes said in an aside, barely moving his lips. "Trust me."

"Fat chance."

But before Tripp could teleport away, Storm was stroking Elara's cheek. The cracked and bleeding lips of a moment before were rapidly healing, and although still asleep, a relieved look settled on Elara's face. Her visage took on a relaxed quality, and she turned her head toward the cooling hand.

"Why is she this way?" Storm asked with a dark frown. "Who did this to her?"

"She's transitioning from a mortal witch," he said.

"Give her to me."

His arms tightened. "What is the pri—"

"No fee will be required. As this fool indicated, I owe him a favor." Storm's ice-gray eyes flashed with her anger as she cut Hermes a surly glance. "However, I'd never let another nymph suffer, favor or no."

Still, he had to know. "What is it you intend to do with her?"

"I'll provide her with what she needs to survive." Her gaze was assessing as she watched him, waiting for him to decide.

"How long will you hold her? We have a bit of a situation that needs resolving back home."

Black brows shot skyward, and she looked between Hermes and him.

"What has he done now?" she asked with a tilt of her head toward his cousin.

"The boots on Elara's feet. His curse on us."

Hermes took exception. "Now, wait a damned minute! Those boots were a gift from your mother, not me."

"Yes, yes, yes. You're only hanging about to make sure Elara and I don't screw up in this lifetime." Tripp shot him a dirty look. "I got it."

With a careless shrug, Hermes crossed his arms and surveyed the bay. "Nice place you have here, Stormy Baby."

She snorted, but there was humor in the sound. Turning back to Tripp, she asked? "Enguerrand Nightshade, yes?"

"Yes," Tripp confirmed.

"And who is the woman?"

"Elara Hawthorne."

"Hawthorne!" Storm's brows shot upward again, and her expression was one of astonishment. "One of Helios's?"

"A descendant, yes," Hermes confirmed. However, there was a sketchy quality in his voice, as if yet another surprising revelation awaited Tripp.

"What are you not telling us?" she asked his cousin. Without waiting for a reply, she said, "Enguerrand, give Elara to me and step back, please."

At six feet tall, Storm's build was impressive. Her body possessed not an ounce of fat, and her movements highlighted her sinewy muscles as she reached forward.

He glanced around for the first time, realizing they were in the Amazonian jungle. "You're the queen here?" he asked, gently placing Elara in her arms and hesitating to move backward in case the weight was too much for her. It wasn't, and she easily held Elara's petite form.

"No, but my daughter is. I'm the wise woman for her people."

"Your reputation is scary for a wise woman."

The flash of her pearly white teeth startled him. "That's more for *our* kind than for the villagers here. This land should remain untouched."

"Yet the humans are encroaching and stripping the land," Hermes said with a scowl.

Storm nodded. "Yes, but as long as I live, this area shall always be protected."

"Your secret is safe with me," Tripp assured her.

"Excellent." She turned to leave, Elara cradled in her arms.

"Wait!"

Looking back over her shoulder, she cocked her head. "What is it, Enguerrand? The delay is costly."

"How long? What is needed to help her? I—" Breathing became difficult at the thought of Elara out of his sight and reach, should she need him. Hermes's warning about the abduction came back to haunt him.

Understanding and compassion flashed on Storm's regal visage. "Fear not, demigod. She is in good hands. I'll not allow anything to happen to her. Return to the water's edge in seven hours, and she shall be waiting."

Before he could offer any other questions, she sank to the bottom of the clear bay, taking Elara with her. As the whirlpool started in the center, it took every ounce of willpower and Hermes's grip to keep him from diving in after them.

"Don't!" His cousin gave him a hard shake. "She'll be fine, but you won't be if you enter the bay without permission."

"I can't leave her," Tripp croaked. His heart felt torn from his body, and his chest ached as he strained to see Elara through the swirling depths.

"Sit and wait if you must, but don't you dare go into the water."

He nodded his agreement, backed a few feet, and sank onto the sun-warmed sand. "Do you know what she'll do to cure her?"

"No, but I have an idea."

Tripp raised a brow, expecting Hermes to elaborate.

He didn't.

"You're an asshole."

Hermes grinned. "So I've been told."

"When this is over, remind me to punch you in the face."

CHAPTER TWENTY

Tripp Nightshade.

He was all Elara dreamed about in her fevered state. The memories of her past lives returned to her with the wash of power flooding her cells, and she recalled the times they'd met and were crazy hot for each other. In each lifetime, she'd fallen for him, but he'd never proclaimed his love.

Disaster had followed.

Every. Single. Time.

Her eyes snapped open.

Just as it would this one last time.

The thought felt like a certainty her mind couldn't erase. Following it was the awareness the people of Witchmere were doomed. Instead of celebrating a holiday of love, light, and joy, they'd be fleeing in terror. Their screams of fear would drown out the sound of sleigh bells. No shoppers would rush home with their presents. Instead, they'd rush to escape a town overcome with lava, ash, and toxic air.

Tears streamed from her eyes, soaking her temples and the feather-soft pillow cradling her head. A cool hand stroked her brow, and she shifted to see the woman beside her.

Compassion shone in her light-gray eyes. "How do you feel, sister?"

"Like I could drink an ocean, and it still wouldn't be enough? Why am I so thirsty?"

"A lifetime spent denying your heritage. It will pass soon."

"Heritage?" Elara frowned, struggling to recall what she'd heard at the meeting. "Water nymph."

"Yes. Fathered by a Titan."

"No, he's my three-times great-grandfather or something like that."

The woman laughed. "Is that what they told you?"

Elara nodded.

"They lied."

"I don't understand," she said. "If my parents were gods, I'd know."

The gray eyes narrowed in contemplation. "Let me guess. The story goes something like this: Your father was loving and indulged your flighty mother's every whim. But they never stayed in one place for long."

Elara froze.

The guess was accurate and eerie as hell.

"I can tell by your shocked expression that I'm right." The woman sighed and stroked her cheek. "Sorry, little one, but your parents were not mere mortals. Mother of nymph descent, Titan father. The power radiating off of you is a testament to this fact."

Rolling her head to stare at the ceiling and consider what the other woman had said, Elara was struck by another realization. She gasped and jackknifed into a sitting position.

"We're in a bubble under the water?"

"We are."

"How? Where?"

"I suppose I should introduce myself. I'm Storm. You're half-sister."

Elara's head almost came off her shoulders; she whipped it around so fast. "What? Half-sister?"

"Same father."

"Rupert Hawthorne is your dad?"

Her newfound sister snorted. "Rupert? Is that what he's calling himself now?"

"Please, I am completely in the dark on this one. Can you give me the highlights here?" The pleading in her voice was cringeworthy, but she'd had the week from hell and needed the clarification.

"Of course."

The woman unfolded herself from the bed and rose, revealing a tall, perfectly toned body. It came as a surprise to realize she was naked.

"Do you, uh, normally walk around in that state?" Cheeks hot, Elara gestured up and down.

As if she had just registered her nudity, the woman laughed. "Yes. I forget it bothers others."

"I'm not bothered. I—"

"It's not what you're used to?"

"Yes." Elara sighed in relief, feeling understood despite the situation's bizarreness and the inability to communicate properly.

"Not to worry." With a snap of her fingers, her sister was clothed in a sheer, flowing robe. The peek-a-boo material showed nearly every ounce of her gleaming, dark-brown skin. "Better?"

"Um…"

Deep-throated laughter rang out, and Elara recognized she was being teased.

Another snap and the sheerness of the robe was gone, effectively covering all the exposed bits women normally hid in their modesty.

"Sorry, but your face was too priceless for words." The woman leaned in and kissed Elara's hot cheek. "You're adorable, little sister."

"And foolish, I suppose?"

"I wouldn't go that far unless you've lost your heart to the gorgeous demigod who left you on my doorstep."

Her heart sank to the floor of her sister's watery residence. "Tripp left me?"

The watchful gray eyes narrowed slightly. "I see I'm too late to warn you away. And yes, he handed you over to me. However, it wasn't by choice, so you can lose the crestfallen look, dear heart."

"Is he okay?" Pulse-pounding fear for him took root, and Elara jumped to her feet.

"He's fine. See for yourself." Her sister waved a hand, and the mirrored wall Elara had failed to notice before transformed from hazy to clear, showing him. Tripp paced the sandy shoreline, careful to avoid the lapping waves, and every so often, he'd look toward the center of the bay. Concern etched his perfect visage, and it warmed Elara.

With a relieved sigh, she murmured, "He didn't leave me."

"No. Seven hours he's waited, and he'd likely wait seven hundred more. It would take an act of Zeus to remove that man from the shoreline, and still, he'd find a way to return to you," her sister replied in a droll voice. "The fool with him would've gone a long time ago, though."

Elara spotted Hermes napping in the sun a short distance away. "He's not so bad once you get to know him."

"You know him? In what sense?"

The sharpness of her sister's tone caught her attention. The two shared history.

"In the Trickster sense," Elara said. Grimacing, she pointed to her boots. "He's been trying to make sure I don't end the world because of his stupid enchantment."

"Like I said, he's a fool." Anger hardened the woman's face. "He thinks nothing of stirring up trouble, then leaving others to clean up his mess. He's a special kind of—"

"Careful, Stormy, my love." His voice echoed through the chamber, though he hadn't moved from his spot on the sand.

"Holy shit!" Elara squeaked. "How did he do that?"

"Gods possess the ability to tune into frequency. If he knows who and what he wishes to listen to, he can find them and eavesdrop." She raised her voice and called out, "Shitbag!"

His affectionate chuckle filled the room.

"Uh, Stormy, is it?"

"Storm, but yes."

Elara approached the mirror and touched Tripp's image. "How do I get back to him?"

"You should make him stew a little longer. It's good for a relationship."

She laughed, unable not to in the face of her new sister's pique. But just as quickly, her amusement died, and she gave Storm a sympathetic look. "Hermes must've done a number on you."

"He's a careless prick, like the rest of the Gods. They think only of their pleasures and of no one else."

"I'm sorry."

Storm's expression softened. "You have no reason to be, dear heart. You are as much a victim of his games as anyone."

"True." Raising her voice, she called, "Shitbag!"

Storm's laughter blended beautifully with Hermes's as the sound met Elara's ears. Harmonious humor, as it were.

"So, about this shared father who isn't as mortal as I believed," she said. "What can you tell me?"

"The man you know as Rupert Hawthorne is Rhalassar of Hawthorne, son of Helios. No one knows who his mother is, not even our father, but for certain, she was a Goddess." Storm shrugged as if it were an everyday occurrence not to know your parentage. Perhaps in the world of immortals, it was the norm, but it wasn't something Elara would grow used to.

"And *your* mother?"

"Varinnia."

Sadness tinged the spoken name, and though Elara didn't want to pry, she felt she needed to ask. "What happened?"

"Poseidon banished her for consorting with Rhalassar. She was promised to another."

"So she came to your bay to have you?" Elara guessed.

"Yes. My birth brought forth an epic storm here in the Amazon."

"Ah! Hence the name Storm."

"More formally, Storm Bringer," her sister said with a careless shrug. But she couldn't fully disguise her hurt.

"What happened to your mother?"

"She languished, heartbroken and betrayed. When I was barely more than a child, her life force left her, and she transformed into the crystal stalagmite that serves to support my home."

Elara pressed her hands to her mouth, holding back a cry of dismay. It was easy to envision the entire scenario. The man she knew as Rupert Hawthorne would've never thought about leaving his daughter to survive on her own. It's why the story seemed plausible. Also, something about the woman's proud bearing reminded Elara of Payton.

"I'm so sorry," she said. "Both for your loss and for our absent father."

"It's not your fault. And it's not your mother's, either. Between mine and yours, there were many women, and Rhalassar broke hearts aplenty."

"He always made it seem like he had no choice but to follow my 'flighty' mother, but it must've been the other way around."

"Perhaps. Or maybe your mother was one he truly cared for. It matters not after all this time."

Elara shook her head. "How are you so chill about it? I'm sure I'd be furious."

"I suppose it's the one thing I can be grateful to Hermes for. He taught me the Gods are fickle creatures, out for their pleasures. When they receive what they want, they move on."

Hadn't Elara thought the same thing during the meeting?

Movement in the mirror caught her attention. Hermes was sitting upright and glaring toward the bay. "You kicked me out of your bed, Stormy! I didn't leave you."

"Because you're a self-indulgent shitbag!" Storm shouted back.

The ground rumbled, and lightning flashed, causing Tripp to

run toward them. Her sister threw up a hand, and a wall of water blocked his path. At the same time, Hermes tackled him to the sand.

"What the fuck did I tell you about entering the bay?" he shouted at Tripp. "Do you have a fucking death wish?"

"Why can't he enter?" Elara asked her sister.

Storm placed a finger to her lips before creating a secondary bubble to encase the two of them. To test the soundproofing, she hollered. Neither Hermes nor Tripp reacted. With a nod of satisfaction, she said, "Technically, he can, but he might become sick if his intentions aren't pure of heart. My mother cursed these waters, and unless they offer a sacrifice, one cannot enter without permission."

"Sacrifice? What about me?"

"You're different. You're a water nymph—and related to me. You're welcome anytime."

Having been denied loving family relationships all her life, Elara felt tears sting her eyes at the blasé welcome. And when Storm hugged her, those tears flowed unrestrained.

"It's okay, little sister. You're loved."

And hers were the hardest words to hear. Mainly because she found them difficult to believe.

CHAPTER TWENTY-ONE

"What the devil is taking so long?"

Tripp was fit to be tied. It had been over eight hours since Storm had taken Elara into her underwater den, and the wait was killing him. The mini-earthquake sent him charging toward the bay, requiring Hermes to restrain him.

"She's fine," his cousin had growled. "If you're that obsessed with the girl, take a hard look at your feelings, why don't you?"

And with nothing to do but wait, Tripp had. Since the incident, he'd been examining what he felt for her from the first time they'd met in London until now. Considering what he knew of emotions, he'd come to a conclusion.

He loved her.

Perhaps he always had. Her shy glances at his shoulders during their first introduction in Witchmere had sparked his interest, and it had never gone away. Not in over two years. He'd been so busy panicking over those blasted boots that he'd failed to realize he'd fallen deeper than intended this time.

"You're awfully quiet," Hermes commented from the comfort of his spot in the sand. "What gives?"

"I was doing as you suggested and taking a hard look."

"Great. And?"

Tripp cast him a wry smile. "It was a good suggestion."

Hermes grinned and, for once, remained silent.

"How much longer?" Because he was dying to profess his love to her and didn't feel he could wait another bloody minute.

"They're bonding. Give them time."

"Bonding? Who? Elara and Storm?"

"Yes. They're sisters."

Tripp scoffed. "It's a stretch to call water nymphs sisters."

"No. I mean, they're truly sisters," Hermes said. "They share a father, and if you'd shut up for longer than five minutes, I could hear what's going on."

Tripp's jaw dropped. "Hear… What? You can hear them?"

"You could, too, but you haven't tried."

"No. I can pinpoint Elara's location and sense her emotions, but I can't hear her."

"Because you haven't tried," Hermes reiterated. "It's all about frequency and maintaining a calm mind."

"How?"

"Tune into her emotions, leave off your own, and blank your mind. It should be easy since you're all looks and no brain anyway."

"Fuck off."

Theirs was the kind of good-natured relationship that allowed them to dig at each other without getting salty—for the most part. Until Elara, that was. Tripp discovered he was highly sensitive regarding her. It didn't sit well that Hermes posed as Hex for the length of time he had or that Elara had adored the beast.

But Tripp did as he suggested, blanking his mind to listen.

"I should get back," Elara said. *"Tripp and I need to resolve the issue of Rainier before it blows."*

"What do you owe any of those people? Have they been kind to you?" Storm asked. *There was a hint of snideness to her tone Elara chose to ignore.*

"Some," she said. "But either way, I don't want it on my conscience."

"You may go if you wish, but remember to frequent the ocean when you can. You must swim often to rejuvenate your nymph cells and feed the magic."

"I'll remember. Will you visit me? I'd love for you to meet our sister, Payton."

"I'd be honored."

"Um, how do I get to the surface?" Elara asked hesitantly.

"You merely think about your destination, and you're there."

"Really? It's that easy?"

"It's that easy," Storm assured her. "Look into the mirror. See Enguerrand waiting for you? Imagine yourself beside him, and there you'll be."

And there she was. Tripp was never so happy to see anyone in his life, and he hauled her into his arms, holding onto her like a safety line.

"I thought I'd lost you," he said roughly. "Between the fever, my mother's abduction scheme, and Storm taking you to the watery depths of her bay…"

Drawing back, she stared at him in wonder. "Are you admitting to feelings, Tripp Nightshade?"

"Yes."

And because he couldn't wait, he kissed her. The action was more satisfying, as if acknowledging his love for her, even if it was only to himself, made her touch transformative, drawing him in deeper. She tasted sweeter, the air smelled purer, and his heart was lighter.

"I hate to break up this lovefest, but we need to return to Witchmere," Hermes said. "We have a volcano to appease."

Tripp never wanted to part from her, but his cousin was right. He drew away and caressed her kiss-swollen lips with his fingertips. "We need to talk. Soon. Just the two of us."

Expression troubled, she nodded, and he wondered what he'd missed. Had Storm revealed some tidbit of information that would affect their relationship? He hoped not.

"I want to go home," Elara said. "I'll meet you there."

"Wait!" But she was gone, and it occurred to him she'd learned to teleport in the last few minutes. "Shit!"

"She's a fast learner," Hermes said, smiling like a proud parent.

"Stuff it." Picturing her living room, Tripp teleported. But she hadn't arrived, and his concern ratcheted up. If she had one stray thought in the process, she might be in Timbuktu.

The apartment door opened, and Payton walked in. "Oh, thank the Goddess! I've been calling Elara all day. Everyone has been looking for you—where is she?" She charged into the bedroom and, from there, the small bathroom, then returned to glance out the French doors leading to the porch. "Where's my sister, Tripp?"

"I don't know," he confessed. "She told me she'd meet me here, and when I arrived, it was to an empty apartment. I got here a few minutes before you." He ran a trembling hand through his hair. "I'm worried, too."

"We have to find her! Your mother came up with some insane idea to abduct her."

"Hermes told me. If you give me a moment of silence, I can locate her."

"How?"

Tripp raised a brow and mimed zipping his lip. Although she scowled, Payton nodded and complied.

Shutting his eyes, he tuned in to Elara's unique energy and sighed in relief. "Across town. She's speaking with Harrison Cobb."

"One day, you'll have to tell me how you do that."

"I will. More importantly, I'll show you when you come into your power."

She opened her mouth to speak, but shook her head and stalked toward the door.

"It's faster if we teleport. Hold my hand."

They arrived in the alley across the street from Harrison's office building. From his vantage point, Tripp could see Elara inside, her arms flailing as she spoke. Other than the occasional startled expression, the therapist nodded and let her vent.

And vent, she did. Thanks to his new ability to listen in, Tripp heard everything and had mixed emotions about what he should do.

"I'll leave you here," he told Payton. "Your sister has much to tell you."

"Where are you going?"

"To the lake. I need to think without everyone in my business."

Elara exited Harrison's office to find Payton loitering on the bench outside. She was chewing her fingernail with a restless energy that screamed high alert.

"Payton? What's going on? Are you okay?"

"Elara!" Her sister hugged her so tightly that Elara had difficulty breathing.

"Loosen... up," she gasped.

"Sorry. It's just with Brenda of Messing—"

"Brelenia of Messia," Elara corrected.

"Yeah, whoever, whatever. She was concocting mad schemes to kidnap you—"

"Kidnapping is for children. Abduction is for adults."

Payton glared. "Why the hell aren't you listening and taking this seriously?"

"Because I don't care about all that garbage. You and I need to talk. I have a lot to share." Elara grabbed her hand and dragged her toward the *Mystic Macarons & More* bakery. If she didn't eat something soon, she'd grow hangry and set off the fucking volcano out of spite.

The fragrant smell of baked goods greeted them, and her stomach rumbled louder than the last earthquake.

"A coffee and a dozen key lime macarons, please. Add whatever she wants to my order." She gestured to Payton with her thumb.

"A dozen?"

"Don't judge. Shit got real."

"Fair. I'll have the same, but lemon chiffon macarons, please," Payton told the cashier.

Other than a raised eyebrow, the bakery worker said nothing and rushed off to fill their order. Once they'd paid and were seated, her sister demanded details.

"What's going on?"

"Remember the meeting? The fever and all that?"

Payton scowled. "Of course. It only happened this morning."

"Yeah, right. Sorry. It feels like it's been a week." Elara sipped her coffee, devoured a key-lime concoction, and cleared her throat. "We have another sister. A half-sister," she said.

Coffee midway to her lips, Payton stared. "What?"

"Her name is Storm Bringer, and she's a badass water nymph in the Amazon jungle."

"Elara, don't take this the wrong way, but what the fuck are you smoking? And where do I get some?"

"I'm serious! Ask Tripp. He's the one who took me there." She shook her head and inhaled another macaron. Stress eating was a real issue for her. "Our father's true name is Rhalassar, and he's the son of Helios, *not* the great-however-many-times-grandchild."

"What?"

"And he was a player! With as many women as he's stuck it to, we might have enough siblings to start a colony."

"That sounds extreme." Payton frowned and consumed two cookies as she processed the information. "He seemed devoted to Mom."

"I thought so, too. Storm seemed to think Mom was the only reason he ended the wild oat sowing."

"Do you think it's why they left Witchmere? Were they on the run or something?"

Elara shrugged. "How the hello-fuzzy would I know?"

"I think we need to question Granny Flo and find out what the hell she's hiding." Payton's chin was raised in challenge as if she expected opposition to her idea. And in the past, Elara might've put the brakes on interrogating Florence, but she was done with people lying to her.

"I agree. Finish your coffee, and let's go."

"You seem different," Payton said during their short walk to *Never Too Many*.

"I'm just tired of others meddling in my life and making decisions without my consent."

Like the damned boots.

She glanced down in time to see the sun catch one of the jewels, and the colorful purple burst eased some of her anger. They were beautiful, and it was hard to be pissed at inanimate objects, though it could be argued that they had a life of their own. Primarily, she was furious at Hermes and Brelenia. At all the Gods in general for their games. Unfortunately, Tripp fell under the subheading of a god, and it was difficult to be around him in her current state.

She couldn't shake the feeling that he, like her father, had been around for hundreds of years and might've been careless with hearts along the way. In her earlier incarnations, he was kind and caring, but he never mentioned love. Yes, he'd admitted to feelings before kissing her at the bay. But again, was it love or affection? Because the two were vastly different.

"Tripp said he was going to the lake. I got the impression you knew which one," Payton said. There was a gentle understanding in her voice, indicating she was sensitive to Elara's feelings.

How many times had she missed the nuanced tone in the past? How had she failed to credit Payton with empathy?

She halted and placed a hand on her arm. "I'm sorry, Pay."

"For what?"

"For being a shitty sister. For not seeing you were hurting, too, and on a deeper level, because of our parents and the situation with Dailey. I only saw your actions through my crappy-life tinted glasses."

Tears filled Payton's large, lovely eyes, and a sad smile curled her lips. "Thank you, but you were never a shitty sister, El. You were the best. When I needed support, you gave it without fail. Don't place the blame for my failures on your shoulders. That's not fair to you."

"I'm not, but I could've been more understanding and less surly when you needed space to be you."

Undiluted love shone back from Payton's beautiful face. "You were dealing with demons, just like me. The endless hours you've spent with Harrison Cobb were your outlet. One I should've copied. Maybe Dailey and I would've worked out."

"It would've been hard to talk to your fiancé's brother in a professional capacity," Elara said, crinkling her nose. "I couldn't have done it." She hugged Payton. "Thank you for your forgiving heart, Pay. I love you."

"I love you, too."

Embarrassed by the outpouring of emotion, she looked down. The stone that had flared to life earlier was glowing brightly.

"Do you see that?" she asked.

"Yeah, it's weird, isn't it?"

"I think I've figured out what I need to do."

"Which is?"

"Resolve all my issues. Past and present."

Payton shrugged. "That shouldn't be hard, considering how enlightened you are."

"It might be. Mom and Dad would be on the list, and finding them after all this time could be tricky." Another stone flared and died out. Excitement built inside her. "That's it, Payton! That's the key to stopping Rainier from blowing!"

"I don't understand."

"Watch." With each name she listed, a different stone lit then dimmed. All but two. "I don't know of any other unresolved situations or relationships," she said, disheartened that she hadn't figured them all out.

"Harrison might have an idea. And as annoying as I find Florence, she might, too."

"She's closed-mouthed when it comes to our familial relationship. I won't count on her for much." Elara huffed out an irritated breath. "But let's get in there and hold her feet to the fire."

Payton's evil grin didn't bode well for their grandmother. "With pleasure!"

CHAPTER TWENTY-TWO

"You know! Start talking!"

Elara's accusation rang in Tripp's mind louder than church bells sounding in a belfry. Her upset prompted him to abandon his self-reflection and find her. After narrowing down her location, he popped into the alley beside the bookstore.

Bohdan was already there, in his massive beast form, pacing back and forth with raised hackles. Upon sensing Tripp, he whirled around and snapped his dangerous jaws. A wolf during the daylight hours wasn't usual, and he was left to assume stronger magic was at play here.

"Hey, Bo," he said, keeping his voice low and soothing as he eased backward. The last thing Witchmere needed was a feral animal attack. "I'm friend, not foe, remember?"

Shifting rocks alerted him to another presence, and he whirled in time to see Archer, transformed into his gargoyle shape, stomping in his direction.

What the hell was going on?

A wave of unsettling fury washed through him.

Not his, but someone with enough power to alter moods and trigger shifters.

Who?

It came to him in an instant.

A Titan.

More specifically, *Elara*.

"Sorry to do this, fellas, but I don't have time to rumble with you."

So saying, he envisioned steel cages rising from the cobbled road, encasing Bohdan and Archer. They might not hold the mighty beasts for long, but it would be enough time for him to calm Elara and have her reverse the enchantment she was unknowingly weaving.

He'd almost reached the door when claws ripped down his back. The searing pain caused him to cry out, and the release of his surprised shout sent out an explosion of energy. Shingles along the rooftops lifted as if fans were performing a stadium wave, and decorative shutters rattled before tumbling to the ground.

Tripp spun back to confront Archer. "I see my cage couldn't hold you."

The gaping mouth was nothing more than a grotesque grin, with teeth as sharp as those damned curled claws he'd raked down Tripp's back. Archer was preparing for another attack.

Tripp had two choices: Stay and fight, or permanently incapacitate the gargoyle. He hated the second option, but there was no time for the first.

One life or the many.

No contest. Tripp would always sacrifice the one for the many —unless that person was Elara.

Holding up his hands, he called forth the elements of wind and water, merging them into an arrow-sized waterspout. "Sorry to do this to you, friend, but you left me no choice."

He threw the arrow straight at Archer's chest, blasting him apart. Boulders rolled in every direction, and Tripp dodged razor-sharp nails and teeth as they flew through the air. Shoving down his sorrow for the loss of the ancient gargoyle, he dashed through the doorway.

The pulsing purple wall was a surprise, and he felt his way along it, following to see where it might end. On his journey through the bookstore, he noticed patrons frozen mid-action, reading or pulling items from shelves. Some who'd sensed the coming storm were locked mid-run, prepared to flee.

Elara had no idea of her power, and Tripp had to warn her before she seriously hurt someone. Archer was on him, and if or when she discovered his fate, Tripp wouldn't let her blame herself.

Once again, he quieted his mind and felt for her.

Office.

Drawing his ancient magic around him like a cloak, he trudged through the ever-thickening wall she'd created. His protection spell was useless, and his flesh burned as wave after wave of her rage struck him. Blood flowed freely down his back from Archer's strike, weakening him.

About five feet from the doorway to the room, he found Hermes. He, too, looked like he'd traveled through hell to get there. Bloody and bruised, his left eye—the one not swollen shut—locked on Tripp.

"I'm sorry."

"For?" Dread was building at the finality in Hermes's voice. He would only apologize for one thing: Elara's death. "No! Let me talk to her."

"Zeus has spoken."

"I don't give a shit. You're not killing my mate!"

A sly smile curled Hermes's bleeding mouth. "Then get your ass in there and stop this."

"Dick!"

"Trickster," his cousin replied. Sighing, he slumped against a shelf and slid to a sitting position. "Hurry, man. I can't contain her magic in this shop much longer."

"It's already seeped out. Out-of-control shifters are converging in the alley."

Hermes shook his head. "Not from her, they aren't. Don't know whose power is stirring them up, but it isn't Elara's."

Tripp didn't have time to figure it out as he dashed toward the storeroom.

When he skidded through the open doorway, Elara and Payton were confronting Florence, who resembled a cornered rabbit ready to bolt.

Acting on instinct, he wrapped an arm around Elara's waist, drawing her back against his chest. "Listen to me, flitter-mouse. You need to let this go. Whatever you think you're doing here, it's the exact opposite. The containment spell you're unleashing is creating chaos."

She tilted her head back, and her startled blue eyes locked with his. "What do you mean?"

"Time within the shop has been suspended, and shop customers are locked in place." Dipping down, he rubbed his nose against hers. "You've got to take a deep breath and approach this conversation with Florence in a rational manner. Remember, the volcano is active beneath us, love."

With a suspicious frown, she looked beyond him to the main desk. Her eyes widened, and she tightened her grip on his arms.

"I did that?"

"You and Hermes. He's doing his damnedest to contain your anger to just the shop."

"Holy shitballs!" Payton exclaimed.

"Yeah," Tripp agreed, never taking his gaze from Elara. He kissed her temple. "Try to clear your mind and breathe in, then out again for the count of five. Can you do that for me?"

Her nod was jerky, as was her inhale. The exhale was smoother but still shaky.

"Good. Again," he urged. After two more rounds of coached breathing, Tripp could feel the enchantment diminishing. "Excellent. Now, how about you and I walk down to *Wily Witches* for coffee?"

"My grandmother needs to tell us what she knows, Tripp. She lied. Rupert isn't any old descendant of Helios. He's his son."

Tripp jerked, feeling lightheaded. "Son? Which one?"

"Rhalassar."

He'd never heard the name, but it didn't mean anything. Helios produced offspring as if it were his personal mission to repopulate the world. But the news made Tripp see Elara in a new light. Her Titan abilities were second generation, and that power made her extremely dangerous to anyone who incurred her wrath.

Him included.

"I told the gel; this is news to me, Nightshade," Florence said, flipping open her cigarette case and selecting one from the remaining three. "I got the information through my daughter, Mae."

The beauty of being a demigod was the ability to discern truth among lies, along with intent. "Florence speaks the truth, flittermouse," he said gently. "I can sense it, and so can you if you listen with your heart."

Elara focused on Florence. "How do I do that?"

"Set aside your preconceived opinions and clear your head of what you've heard. Take her hand and ask your most pressing question. Let the truth wash over you."

With a nod, she patted his arm, and he released her.

"You're a human lie detector now, love. You've got this," he assured her.

Determination on her beloved face, she approached Florence, stopping only a foot away. She held out her hand. "Are you willing to try?"

"I'll tell you the truth, gel. I owe you that much."

Hands clasped, they had an open dialogue. With every probing question Elara or Payton asked, Florence responded with the truth as she knew it.

"Do you know where my father is now?"

"I don't, but I suspect as far away from Olympus as he could get." The older woman drew back and fumbled for another cigarette, eventually remembering the unlit one tucked in the corner of her mouth. "He left here in a hurry with you gels when you were just out of diapers."

"What about our mother? She was with him for a time."

"She found *him*, not the other way around. I don't know if it was prearranged, but Rupert hightailed it with you and Payton, not Mae." The sincere eyes eating up her granddaughter's expressions were filled with sorrow. "She'd been helping me in the shop that day. Rupert had assured her he'd care for the two of you, easing her fears about leaving you gels alone with him. When she returned home, it was to find he'd absconded with both of you and a special artifact they'd kept on the mantle."

"Was it a blue globe with a smaller replica of the Earth in the center?" Payton asked, her brows drawn together in memory.

"Yes."

"A transporter," Hermes said from behind Tripp. "Only three exist, though they were once plentiful. The Titans used them to open portals between continents and dimensions."

"Who has the other two?" Elara asked.

"No one knows, but it was believed Helios hoarded them."

"Is it possible my father has them all?"

"Possible, yes. Probable?" He gave a "meh" shrug.

"He had to have at least two," Elara said, pressing her fingers to her temples. "Our mom had one when she showed up."

"How could you know that, gel?" Florence asked skeptically. "You were far too young."

"I remember everything." Wide, china-blue eyes danced over Tripp's face before dropping to stare at her boots. "Every second of every lifetime I've ever had."

"Holy shitballs!" Payton grinned. "That's badass."

"Not really." The gaze Elara turned on them was filled with pain. "It's a fucking curse to know you've never been enough."

Tripp's heart sank as the mountain rumbled.

"But you are, flitter-mouse. You always have been."

Her twisted smile reeked of sadness. "Not for you."

"Especially for me," he assured her. "You've never been the problem, Elara Elizabeth Hawthorne. I have."

A series of ferocious roars cut through the air, chilling Tripp's blood.

"What the hell is that?" Payton gasped.

"Gargoyles. They want revenge for their leader," he said grimly.

Elara gripped his forearm as more bellows rent the air. "Revenge? What leader?"

"Archer Roche."

"What happened to Archer?" they all asked him in stereo.

"I killed him."

CHAPTER TWENTY-THREE

Tripp Nightshade.

Murderer.

Though not by choice.

Still, from the time he'd announced he'd killed Archer, a lead weight had settled in Elara's belly and refused to budge. She hadn't known the man, but he'd seemed like a quiet, gentle giant. Until she'd gotten a good look at Tripp's shredded back. The entire time he'd been trying to calm her and teach her to control her energy, he'd been wounded. Suffering on her behalf.

Elara wrung out the washcloth and dabbed at the gash as gently as she could while doing her damnedest not to notice the contoured muscles under her hand. It wasn't the time to lust over his perfect body when he was in pain.

"Are you all right, Tripp?" she asked softly.

He took his time answering. "Yeah."

Although she couldn't say how, she sensed the lie. Perhaps she *was* a human lie detector he'd declared her to be.

"You're not." She stroked back his thick, dark hair with her free hand, exposing his profile. "I'm sorry."

"It's not your fault."

"It is," she argued without heat.

Whatever she'd called up to make the supernatural residents crazy had created a short-lived battle between two formidable men, resulting in the loss of life for one. She'd darted past Tripp to confront the gargoyle gang, but they'd transformed back into humans by the time she'd arrived outside.

Hermes misdirected them on Tripp's behalf, allowing them to escape to her apartment.

Tripp half rolled to meet her gaze. "Listen to me, flitter-mouse. Whatever happened in that alley wasn't your fault. Inside the building, yes. Outside was something else. Some*one* else. I wouldn't lie to you."

"But you just did when you claimed to be all right." She managed to keep the censure from her voice and merely stated what she knew to be true.

"True," he agreed. With a self-deprecating grin, he said, "My back aches like a bitch, and I'm concerned it hasn't healed yet."

"Yet? It's only been an hour."

"I heal in minutes, Elara. This new development is concerning."

"Either you're losing your magic, *or*..." She didn't know what the second reason could be. The first was scary enough.

"Or Archer's claws were dipped in a poison," he concluded grimly.

"Which ones might hurt you?"

"Few. Witch's bane would make me sick but not kill me, and I avoid it when I can."

Having never been required to study the basics as any standard witch might, Elara's knowledge of poisonous herbs was woefully lacking. "What about your mother or Hermes? Might they know what could take down a demigod?"

"Probably. I would, too, if my brain wasn't fuzzy." His eyes drifted shut after a series of heavy-lidded blinks. "I'm going to rest, then I'll give it more thought," he murmured.

"Tripp?" When she received no answer, she shook him. "Tripp?"

Nothing.

Not a murmur or a muscle twitch.

"Enguerrand!" she shouted.

Again, no response.

"Hermes!" she thundered. "Get your ass here, now!"

His arrival was instantaneous.

"What the fuck? Why do you keep—Tripp?" His scowl transformed into a disturbed frown. "Did you slip him something?"

"Hell no! Besides, I wouldn't know what to give him. That's why I called you. I'd hoped you could tell me." Elara lifted the gauze from his back. "Archer did this while in his gargoyle form, and Tripp's not healing. These scratches are looking angrier by the minute."

"Having never fought one, he might not know, but Gargoyles distribute a toxic venom through scratches and bites. It's lethal to humans, but gods should be immune."

"Isn't he technically half-human? Would that half be susceptible to the toxin?" she asked.

"Possibly." Hermes appeared perplexed and as worried as she felt. "We have to call Brelenia."

Hating the idea of bringing his meddlesome mother into their business, Elara agreed all the same. If there was poison in Tripp's system that could be neutralized or extracted, she had to take the chance Brelenia could do it.

"Make the call."

The words were hardly out of her mouth before the Goddess stood beside the bed.

"What happened to my son?" Brelenia demanded.

Elara felt the woman's rage to her pinky toes and beyond. "When he was trying to get into the bookstore, he was attacked by Archer Roche. He's a gargoyle."

Bending, his mother examined the wounds. "This wasn't Archer's doing."

"You knew him?"

"Know. His mission has always been to protect."

"Tripp killed him," Elara admitted, with pain in her heart for Witchmere's premier protector. "He—"

"Didn't," Brelenia said.

"What?"

"Archer is perched atop your building, dear. Step outside and see if you don't believe me."

She smiled, and her kindness set off an ache in Elara's heart. What must it be like to have such a caring mother? Yes, recalled memories gave the impression Tripp avoided his mom whenever possible, but Elara also understood that Brelenia's actions were born from her love for him. Whatever she had done, these damned boots included, it was her misguided motherly attempt to make him happy.

"I believe you," she found herself saying. "But if it wasn't Archer, who was it?"

The Goddess sent Hermes a commanding glance. "Find out, please."

"On it."

Then, she was alone with Tripp's mother, suddenly terrified.

"You don't need to fear me, dear," the Goddess assured her as she removed her overcoat and rolled her sleeves. It belatedly occurred to Elara that the outfit blended with those worn by the townsfolk. No one looking at Brelenia would see anyone other than a classy, well-dressed woman.

"How often do you visit the mortal world?" Elara asked, gesturing toward the clothes. "And what can I find you to treat Tripp's back?"

"Often, and nothing but fresh water, please."

She ran to fill the kettle but halted when Brelenia's hands covered hers.

"Not like that, dear. Utilize your elemental magic to conjure what I need."

"Won't it be easier to turn on the faucet?" Elara asked.

"Yes, but then the liquid won't possess the special healing power only you, a water nymph, can create."

All the cupboard doors opened, and an invisible hand plucked two five-quart mixing bowls from the upper shelves. They settled on the counter, ready to be filled.

"Place a palm over the opening of each bowl," Brelenia instructed.

"Like this?" Elara centered her hands two inches above the lip.

"Precisely like that." The Goddess beamed like she was the brightest of pupils. "Now, concentrate on your power. At first, it will seem strange. However, you'll find the nymph cells within you differ from those of your Titan."

"How?"

"They'll be thirsty."

Initially, Elara didn't understand, but the more she centered herself and looked inward, the more aware she became of her body's workings. There were two distinct forces within her, and after a few minutes, she isolated her nymph.

"I found it!" she cried, excited to have someone teach her and hopeful she might help Tripp.

"Excellent." Brelenia waved her hand, and the French doors swung wide. "A snowstorm is brewing. Draw the moisture from outside and add it to the bowls."

"I don't—"

"Concentrate, dear. Feel the cooler air. Sense the droplets in the clouds overhead."

As if hypnotized, Elara felt her entire demeanor calm, and she closed her eyes, doing as instructed. Her body wanted to drink in the dampness to hydrate itself, but she stopped short of giving in to the gluttonous urge. Lifting her lids, she was shocked to see the shimmering water balls hovering just beyond her reach. She fumbled and quickly dove to recover them. When she straightened, she felt like a talented Cirque de Soleil performer and beamed in delight.

"I'm doing it," she crowed, awed she could.

"Yes, my dear girl, you are." The deep satisfaction in Brelenia's voice caught Elara's notice, and she sent her a sharp glance. But the only emotion reflected back was a pride similar to hers. "Now, guide the liquid to the bowls."

Visualizing was the key to all magic, and Elara imagined the water cradled by the ceramic. For once, her spellwork was successful, with no fumbling or screwing up on her part. The liquid went right where she directed it.

"Very good, darling girl. Next, you will remove the impurities." Her dismay must've shown because Brelenia patted her arm. "I'll guide you."

A clock ticked in the back of Elara's mind, making her hyperaware of Tripp's slumbering form in pain. But his mother refused to be rushed, taking precious time to teach her the proper way to perform each task. When they were done, the Goddess gave her one bowl, grabbed the other, and then led her to the bedroom.

"Follow my lead. Scoop a bit of water up and slowly disperse it over his back. Like this." After demonstrating, she nodded to Elara. "Your turn, dear." She smiled after Elara completed her task. "Excellent. Now, scoop more, but place it on his back this time and hold it there. The consistency should be gel-like, contacting his skin from shoulder to hips."

"Like this?" Elara created a cooling gel and layered it on Tripp's open wounds, keeping her arms spread to encompass the width and length of his torso.

"Perfect. Do you think you can maintain that until he's healed?"

"I can try."

Brelenia narrowed her eyes and opened her mouth as if she wanted to say something. After a second's pause, she nodded. "Do your best, please."

"Why is my water nymph magic so important to his healing? Isn't your power stronger?"

"I understand that Enguerrand and Hermes brought you to Storm Bringer's Bay, yes?"

"Yes," Elara said, watching her closely for any sign of displeasure.

"And your fever was helped by the Storm Bringer's magical water, yes?"

"Uh-huh."

Brelenia was making a point and wouldn't be hurried. "Water nymphs, such as the two of you, possess a far greater ability to heal. Water is life."

"I still don't get it. I'm sorry."

"Your parents will get a piece of my mind if ever they return here. It's shameful they denied you the proper tutelage."

The Goddess huffed out a breath when Elara said she was sorry again. Waving off a third apology, Brelenia continued her explanation. "The brain and heart are comprised of roughly seventy-three percent water, while the lungs are higher, at eighty-three percent. Each organ demands its fair share. Even bones require water." She gestured to the closing wounds. "The poison was acidic. And do you know what neutralizes acid?"

"Water."

"Precisely. Water is life. It is healing. Without it, we would all die."

Elara nodded. "Is that why the volcano issue is such a big deal? Because the heat, flames, and lava flow will dissolve and evaporate the mountain's snow and suck the moisture from the air?"

"Partially. It's the ash and lack of oxygen that will kill the people here."

"Yes. But *you* can stop it, right?"

"No, dear. *You* can."

"I don't know how," Elara admitted, feeling stupid and miserable for her part in the threat to Witchmere.

"When the time comes, you'll possess the knowledge. I promise."

She wanted to cry. Why did everyone have to be so damned vague?

"Because you need to sort these things for yourself, dear. You and Enguerrand are two highly intelligent individuals, and between you, you have what it takes to save your little village of Witchwood."

Unaware she'd spoken aloud, Elara jolted when Brelenia answered. Losing some of the slushy water and almost undoing all the hard work she'd managed so far with Tripp's wounds made her eyes burn with tears of frustration.

"Witchmere," she corrected with a sniffle.

Brelenia's lips twitched, and Elara guessed the Goddess had purposely goaded her with the wrong name. What was it Tripp said about the Gods testing mortals?

"Even water nymphs need a little fire inside them, my dear," Brelenia said, patting her cheek in a motherly fashion. "You have more than most, but you have to dig to find it. I suspect, like a volcano, yours isn't far below the surface. But it can bubble up and consume you if you don't learn to manage it."

CHAPTER TWENTY-FOUR

Tripp's body was on fire, and he wanted his misery to end—until he heard Elara speak.

"Can we create a box or bubble to contain his power?" she asked. "The quakes are getting worse."

"He's coming round," his mother said. "All will be well as soon as he wakes."

"How do you—"

He groaned and arched his back, connecting with someone's hand. A deluge of water soaked him and the mattress beneath him.

"Oh!" Elara flushed. "Damn it! I was doing so well."

"You did an excellent job, my dear. The skin has healed, and the rest is up to him," Brelenia assured her. "He's able to manage any residual pain."

The rustle of movement woke him fully, and Tripp shoved back the curtain of hair obstructing his view in time to witness his mother hug Elara. Their affection was visible in the yellow cloud of their merging magic.

While he slept, the two had bonded as friends.

It didn't bode well for him.

Elara placed a palm on his forehead, pronouncing him cooler.

"What happened?" He rolled to a sitting position and rested his hands on her hips to keep her from running away.

"Please stay, flitter-mouse," he urged in a low voice, sensing her intent to bolt.

"A beast, posing as Archer Roche, scratched you," his mother stated.

"Posing as… It wasn't Archer? Are you positive?" The gargoyle had been identical to him, except for the rage-filled energy. Roche wasn't prone to getting overly excited. Neither was Bohdan, for that matter.

Large booted feet entered his periphery, and Archer answered for himself. "A rogue gargoyle, glamoured to look like me, and another to impersonate Bohdan." He held up the severed heads, missing half their faces. Luckily, there was no blood or brains to leak out.

Elara leaned in and whispered, "Isn't it weird the insides are solidified, too?"

Although not quite rock-like, what should've been liquid or jellied was solidified. "Yes."

"It opens the door to *so* many questions," she said with a glance at Archer's crotch.

Fighting the urge to laugh, Tripp buried his face against her abdomen to hide his amusement. When Elara meeped her surprise, he chuckled. Her hands, gripping his head, tightened, but then she recalled others were present. Ever proper, she tugged his hair until they separated.

"Spoilsport," he murmured.

"Behave, Enguerrand. Not all women wish to be mauled in the presence of others." Brelenia sighed as if his bad behavior was the bane of her existence.

Elara's fingers dug into his scalp, and he felt her urge to pull him close. "Oh! No! I don't mind."

The chorus of laughter caused her cheeks to flush in that

adorable fashion, making him want to sweep her up and steal her away for eternity.

"Oh!" she chirped her distress.

Tripp gave her hips a light squeeze to gain her attention. "Ignore them, flitter-mouse. Concentrate on me."

Her blush deepened, and through their physical touch, the images in her mind were transferred to his.

It was highly inappropriate considering the company of others, as was his sudden arousal.

"Everybody out!" he ordered, pulling her onto his lap to hide the evidence of his desire. "We'll meet you in two hours at *Wily Witches*."

Elara hissed his name. "They're going to think we're—"

"Doing what I've wanted to do since I first laid eyes on you?"

He kissed away her objections. The action was like nothing they'd ever shared, and he was immediately lost in the pleasure.

"Enguerrand."

Reprimanded like a schoolboy, Tripp broke away from Elara and sighed heavily. He rested his forehead against hers, and her fevered skin felt too hot against his.

"Damn it, Mother, I thought you'd left. Will you please go away so I can tell the woman I love how I feel?"

"I don't take orders from randy youngsters. You're barely out of the sickbed, darling. So, my intervention was for your own good," she countered.

Elara's lips twitched, and she hid her face against his neck. He had to curb an urge to laugh and groan simultaneously.

"Consider yourself the cold shower for my wayward lust," he replied dryly. "Now, *please*, for the love of Messia, *leave* so I can speak with Elara."

"Show your mother more respect, Tripp," his father said, capturing his attention.

Tripp had been so preoccupied with Elara that he'd failed to register the number of visitors. His responding curse would've been savage, but luckily, she sensed the explosion and clamped a hand over his mouth.

"It's okay," she assured him, exchanging her lips for her palm. The kiss was tender and held promise, but it was tentative, too, as if she didn't quite believe his declaration was legitimate.

"It's not okay. There's much to discuss."

"Yes, but it can wait." Her eyes shone with emotions to match his, but they held excitement, too. "I know how to neutralize the boots, Tripp. It's like Dorothy in the Wizard of Oz, and I've had the power all along."

"Then, let's do it!" He nearly dumped her off his lap in his urgency to rid himself of her fucking footwear.

"It's not that easy. I think it might be a drawn-out process."

She killed his boner and his decent mood with two sentences. "Fuck."

"Watch," she said, sitting beside him on the soaked bed. It dried instantly.

He gaped, and she grinned.

"That's my new party trick, but it isn't what I intended to show you. Watch." The jewels embedded in the leather lit up as she began listing people. With each name, a different stone flared brighter and then dimmed. All but two. "I haven't been able to figure out those. That's what Payton and I were confronting Florence about."

Turning over what he knew about her, he shot a considering glance at his watchful mother. If she knew anything, she wasn't saying, and he'd never get it out of her anyway. If one thumbed through the dictionary's pages until they found "tight-lipped," the first thing they would likely see is Brelenia of Messia's picture.

Tripp looked at his father, who had yet to uncross his arms from the earlier scolding.

Movement in the corner caught his father's eye, and Enguerrand the Second's expression darkened. Following his sightline, Tripp's gaze stopped on Hermes. It seemed dear old Dad had yet to forgive the Divine Trickster for his part in setting off Vesuvius.

Helpful info, that. Tripp's father might be swayed to his side in the coming skirmish for supremacy between mother and son.

Careful to keep his expression neutral, he buried his deepest thoughts. Since Hermes revealed the mind-reading parlor trick, Tripp had understood why his mother was always five steps ahead of him.

"What's next?" he asked them. "Do we have a resolution marathon planned for Elara?"

"Not a bad idea," she said, leaning into his shoulder and providing a united front against his parents and Hermes. "Who is in charge of the stopwatch?"

"That would be those cursed boots and the volcano," his father told her, but his stern visage had softened enough to give her a kind smile. "I suggest making a list and handling the easiest affairs first. Work up to the difficult ones, and you may find they won't be as severe when you get to them."

"Then that's what I'll do, Mr. Nightshade." Her grin rivaled the sun in brilliance. "Thank you," she said prettily. "Every little bit of advice helps."

His father's heart melted. Elara had no way of knowing, but Enguerrand the Second was once a scholar who loved dispensing advice and molding young minds. Her willingness to listen endeared her to him, just as it had Tripp, his mother, Hermes, or anyone who had ever encountered her. No one could hold out against her beautiful soul for long.

"You mentioned things and people from a previous timeline, my dear. How do you plan to tackle those issues?" his mother asked Elara.

"I'm not sure. But I suspect it's not the people so much as the lesson behind the incident." Five stones turned on, radiating a steady light. She looked to Hermes for answers. "Does this mean I've guessed correctly?"

"It does. I'd say your previous lifetime lessons were learned." He winked. "Only six more items to go."

"The ones concerning Tripp and me should be resolved. He said he loved me."

"His deepest feelings weren't in question. The only person he was hiding from was himself." Hermes shot a pointed look at Tripp. "It's the actions associated with the love that matter."

"The commitment," Tripp concluded, wanting to smack himself on the forehead. The *duh* moment almost laid him low. "But we're determined to save this town. How much more committed can I be?"

His mother angrily threw up her hands and exited the room, with her husband on her heels.

He scrubbed his hands over his face. "I'm too tired to figure out what I said wrong. A little help here, please."

Elara took pity on him. "You had the first part correct, but the second isn't about commitment to the town. It's the commitment to your happiness and maybe someone else's."

"That feels more like selfishness to me."

"Your mom wants to see you settled, Tripp. You avoid it for several reasons." She ticked items off using her fingers. "Your past traumas. A rebellious nature. Fear of losing the next great love of your life—"

"*You* are that love, and yes, I fear losing you."

Her insides turned gooey. "I fear losing you, too."

Another stone put on a spectacular light show.

"We're making progress!" Hermes was as giddy as a small child opening presents. "Keep going, kids! I—" He mimed a lip-zip when Tripp shot him a death glare.

"Talk to Harrison," Elara urged. "Maybe bring Brelenia and your dad with you. Resolve a few issues. I need to find mine and do the same."

"I'm not sure I'm comfortable with you wandering off on some quest alone," Tripp admitted. His underlying worry was evident in the tightness around his mouth and dark, worried eyes.

"I'll admit I do better with you as a mediator, but if I promise to take Hermes with me and keep my cool, would it put your mind at ease?"

"My mind will never be at ease with Hermes around," he replied dryly.

"Ouch! I'm offended, cousin. Oops. My bad." Halting his snarky dialogue, Hermes mimed a second lip-zip.

Elara lost it. Hearing an ancient deity use the modern term "my bad" was too much for her, and laughter bubbled up. Both men stared with wondrous smiles on their faces. The instant she sobered, they snapped out of the enchantment. Hermes frowned, and Tripp scowled. He must've realized what she had: their reaction wasn't normal.

"What was that?" she asked curiously. "Why were you in a trance? The boots?"

"Actually, it may be the Titan-water nymph duo," Hermes said, scratching his chest. "You cast an enchantment with your laughter, like you did earlier with your anger."

"She did?"

"I did?"

Elara shared a worried look with Tripp. They were on the same page. "What does it mean? I can't allow emotion to show, or I risk influencing people against their will?"

"Something like that," Hermes replied grimly. "We need to speak with Brelenia and my father."

"That's a huge nope on your dad." She shook her head and held up a hand. "Didn't Zeus hate the Titans? Weren't they a risk or something?"

"No, and yes. But that explanation is much too long to get into."

"I'll get my mother, Hermes. We'll begin there." Tripp rose and exited the room, leaving her alone with his cousin.

"I thought he hated the idea of you and me together," she said, attempting to keep it light.

"With good reason." Winking, he settled on the bed, tucked his arms behind his head, and closed his eyes. "I miss my life as Hex. Want to come pet my fur?"

"Oh, for the love of frog guts! What is *wrong* with you?"

"Too many things to list on those delicate fingers of yours," he said with a laugh.

"Harrison Cobb would have a field day analyzing you. Maybe you and Tripp can get a family discount."

One emerald eye popped open, and his lips curled with his amusement. "Don't tell me there's trouble in paradise now that you've proclaimed your love for Prince Charming."

"Prince… Why did you call him that?" She settled next to him, with her back against the headboard. Staring morosely at her boots, she tapped the tips together.

"If you wish to go home, Dorothy, you need to tap the heels together," he said dryly.

"Hush, you turd."

"Turd? I've been downgraded from 'Shitbag?'" His black brow shot up, and his resemblance to Tripp was more pronounced.

"A small downgrade. I'm still not happy you posed as Hex. Why did you?"

"I suspected Tripp would eventually find you. It's the Fates' design. And it was your last chance with my fabulous footwear."

She snorted. "Tripp calls them 'fatal footwear.'"

"He doesn't understand the beauty of my design."

"I don't either. Why did you curse me?" she asked.

"They were never meant as a curse, love. They were to elevate your magic and give you the courage to act when needed." He rolled onto his side and propped his head on his hand. Smiling, he touched the closest crystal-shaped amethyst dangling from a glittery purple lace. "I like your take on them."

"What do you mean?"

"Every person who opens the box will see a different pair of shoes, depending on their mood. It's a whimsy I built into the enchantment. As I did the sizing." He grinned. "Don't tell Brelenia I said this, but you have daintier feet. Her big boots are her vanity."

"Shut up," she laughed and shoved him. "They are not. She's not vain in that sense."

"Isn't she, though?"

Because he sounded thoughtful, Elara considered it. "I don't think so, but why don't you explain it to me?"

"Her greatest vanity is the *perfect* image she always needs to create. The perfect family, marrying Enguerrand the Dull and producing a passel of children. The perfect oasis, Messia—where the weather is ideal all year, and the people never stop smiling. The perfect son, Tripp." Hermes flicked her knee. "The perfect daughter-in-law."

Unease settled in Elara's breast. "Stop it. You're stirring up your special brand of dog doo. You've been upgraded from Sir Turd to Sir Shit-stirrer."

"I speak the truth. Always."

"With a suggestive tone, as if you have a secret no one else knows." She cast him a sour look. "And I suppose you do. You like to keep things close to your chest."

"I'd like to keep you close to my chest. And other body parts."

"See!" She poked his nose. "That right there. You're a flipping troublemaker, Hermes."

"What has you fired up?" His too-charming grin flashed.

"Maybe the fact that you posed as Hex, and I loved him. But now, I have nothing, and it sucks."

Another jewel flared, and she gaped at him.

"You did that on purpose," she breathed.

His impossibly green eyes turned somber. "I'm invested in the outcome, love. You're Stormy's sister, and she deserves a living connection with you."

"She'll always have it if she wants it." Elara smiled, happy to see another issue crossed off her list. "If the results weren't deadly, I'd recommend everyone get a pair of these gorgeous boots."

He chuckled. "Maybe I'll create a new prototype."

"You'll make millions with your therapy shoes!"

CHAPTER TWENTY-FIVE

As he lingered in the shadow of the entrance, Tripp observed Elara and Hermes. He didn't love how cozy they were, and the urge to smash his cousin's handsome, grinning face balled his fists. Lightning flashed outside, and the following thunder caught their notice.

Elara's entire essence glowed when she saw him, and any jealousy he'd felt melted away, replaced by a sense of well-being.

She loved him.

Just as he loved her.

Their main problem was commitment to one another, and they had less than three days to satisfy the Trickster's curse.

When Tripp opened his arms, she scrambled up and took a running leap from the mattress, embracing him with her whole body. His eyes drifted shut as he absorbed her happiness to see him. Yes, teasing and flustering her had been fun, but her confidence grew exponentially. He could easily spend his life receiving this type of welcome.

"I love you." His voice was low and gruff from the force of his emotions. "It feels good to acknowledge and say it aloud."

Keeping her legs locked around his hips, Elara drew back to

gaze into his face. "It does, but not as good as it feels to hear it. To live it."

"Yes." He grinned. Once again, she'd captured precisely what he'd found difficult to relay. "You'd think, after all the years I've been alive, I'd find a way to express my thoughts as concisely and eloquently as you do."

"When it matters, you can," she assured him with a quick, firm peck. "Hermes helped me clear another block."

He glanced at his cousin, and the longing on Hermes's face disturbed him. Was it for Elara? Had he fallen hard for her, too?

"No, Tripp," Hermes said, having tuned into his thoughts. "It's the experience I want."

He offered up a commiserating smile. For too many years, Tripp had witnessed couples holding hands while shopping, sharing bites of their food, and laughing at inside jokes with their lovers. Those moments created such a profound longing that he'd had to look away. Now, he recognized what he'd been missing was Elara's love.

Another stone flared, and Hermes winked.

"Keep helping us clear those blocks, and I'll name my firstborn after you," Tripp quipped.

Elara shut down. The speed with which she withdrew almost did his head in.

"What did I say?"

"I don't want kids," she blurted. "Not now, not ever."

His parents walked in on her declaration, and his mother's hands flew up to cover her gasp.

Hermes hung his head. "Back to the fucking drawing board."

As he searched his feelings on the matter, his mother protested.

"It's fine." All eyes turned in his direction. Elara appeared tearful and unsure of his response, and her reticence tugged at Tripp's heartstrings. Clasping her hand, he gently pulled her forward, embracing her. "I'm never going to force you to do what you don't want to, flitter-mouse. If you don't wish to have children, we won't."

Her scrunched face told the story of her struggle not to cry. "Really? You're okay with it?"

"I'm okay with it."

"Enguerrand!" His mother's dismay created a heavy atmosphere. "I believed she was ready in this lifetime. I'd have never sent those blasted boots if she wasn't."

Elara's temper sparked to life, and with it, the mountain woke. Outside the patio doors, Rainier's snowcapped peak was shrouded by a blast of ash.

If Tripp couldn't calm her, literal hell on earth would commence. "Elara—"

"I *am* ready, Brelenia," she said through clenched teeth. "Having children or not doesn't mean I can't accept Tripp's love or he mine. Women aren't mindless baby-producing vessels. And if you can't see that, you aren't the person or leader you believe yourself to be!"

"Oh, shit," he, his father, and Hermes chorused.

"I've been around for over two millennia, you disrespectful child!" Brelenia stomped forward, intent on putting Elara in her place. Rage caused her amber eyes to glow gold, and her bejeweled fingers curled into fists. "You were selected for my son to make him happy and procreate. And yes, if that makes you a mindless baby-producing vessel, then you will accept your role as the Gods and the Fates see fit."

"You can all go fuc—"

Tripp covered Elara's mouth, wrapped an arm around her waist, and teleported to his apartment. The earth was in distress, grumbling and groaning, sending his art collection crashing to the floor.

"Elara, I don't want to tell you what to do, but if you don't calm down, you'll kill us all. And if *you* don't, my mother will." He shook her to snap her out of the spell weaving around them. The Trickster magic had merged with her heightened emotions and

Titan magic, creating a problem on an epic scale. "I love you, and you'll always have your agency. Any decisions will be made as a couple, and no one else will have a say."

Her fight for control was valiant, and only the slightest panic showed in her troubled eyes. The building settled, and he looked toward the mountain, glad to see the smoke clearing. But the commotion in the streets below was intensifying, with people pointing and others running for safety. Drawing on his elemental power to influence others, he began the painstaking task of spreading calming energy.

Satisfied he'd done his best, he opened his eyes to find Elara watching him.

"What did you do?" she demanded.

"Remember when you said you do better with me as a mediator?"

She nodded.

"Well, it's one of my special gifts. I'm able to manipulate energy and soothe heightened emotions."

Frowning, she gestured to the window. "Mass hypnosis?"

"Something like that," he said, smiling.

Her brows met in a scowl. "To be clear, you can manipulate people into doing what they don't want. Is that right?"

Too late. He'd fallen into a trap of his own making.

"Elara, please listen."

"No! Not if you're weaving spells into your words!" She clapped her palms over her ears, and her voice was unnaturally loud when she asked, "What happens if you eventually decide you want children? Will you use your influence to change my mind?"

"No!" He pulled her hands away. "I told you, you have agency. Any decisions are mutual, flitter-mouse."

For a prolonged moment, she stared at him, and Tripp held his breath.

"I don't know if I should believe you," she whispered, jerking away. "You're saying you manipulated me in the past."

The ground shook, and a crack formed on Main Street. It matched the one in his heart.

"Don't do this. Please don't question my intentions." He reached for her hands, but she danced backward. "Elara, I promise you, I will always value your opinion and consider your feelings."

"I need time to think," she croaked.

The road's fissure widened, and screams echoed from the street below.

"You know I'd give it to you if I could, but we don't have it." Recognizing the angst in his voice as desperate pleading, he cleared his throat and tried again. "If or when you commit to becoming my lifelong mate, I will transfer the ability to you."

Her jaw dropped. "Gods can do that?"

"Yes, and I'll see it's done."

With a distressed look, she nodded. "I'll think about it."

Tripp Nightshade.

Ever the peacemaker.

Elara weighed his words as she perused the ancient tomes in the *Never Too Many* attic. Would he stick to his promise? What person in their right mind would give their power to another the way he'd offered to do? How could he trust her to do the right thing with so heady an ability?

Spent too much money shopping online? Wave a hand to have your husband assure you it's all right.

Murder your rival? Snap your fingers to have him help you bury the body.

"You're overthinking it," Tripp said, stepping from the shadows.

Her bloodcurdling scream shook the rafters.

"Fire-bellied toad turds! Stop doing that!"

His brows shot up at her bizarre exclamation. "That's a new one."

"Well, yes." She fanned her hot face. "But they're also what I need for the spell to find my parents."

"Excellent." He held out his hand. "This is me, asking without influencing, if you'll take a break and come with me."

She accepted his hand. "Where are we going?"

"To the beach. Although it's stuffy up here, it's in no way hot. I think your water nymph needs refreshment."

"I'd forgotten."

"That's why I'm here. To remind you and provide what you need."

She halted when he would've led them downstairs. Gazing up into his curious visage, she made a decision. "I can commit to a lifetime with you, Tripp, and I don't want your ability." His astonishment made her laugh. "Not what you were expecting?"

"Not after fire-bellied toad turds," he admitted with a chuckle.

"Yeah, it surprised me, too. But you had a good argument."

"May I kiss you and show you exactly how happy you've made me?"

"No." She shrugged under his stare. "I'm too hot. Water first, make-out session second."

"Deal. And when we get to the beach, I want to learn all about this locator spell of yours. I've never come across one requiring fire-bellied toad turds."

The next half hour was lighthearted and lovely as Tripp taught her to manipulate her body's temperature. Once he was satisfied she had the basics, they crossed the parking lot to the beach path.

"Crap! I forgot they only come off when I go to bed." She considered the distance to the water. It wasn't far, but she'd deal with sand in her boots the rest of the day.

"I'll carry you." His gallant offer pulled a girly sigh from her.

But before she could accept, her shoes morphed into purple flip-flops with a massive plastic daisy on each toe thong. They were whimsical and perfect.

"I guess that settles that. Leave it to Hermes to create practical footwear," Tripp said with a wry chuckle.

Like children, they frolicked along the water's edge, with Elara dipping her toes in the Sound when no one was looking. Although not the dead of winter, late December was cold in Washington, and passersby would think she was insane if they saw her.

"We should get back," he said, and Elara detected regret in his voice.

"Will it always be like this, do you think? Will you ever grow tired of me?"

His smile was slow and sweet. "Elara Elizabeth Hawthorne, you can rest assured I will never tire of you. Would I have sought you out in each of your incarnations if I thought I might?"

"But maybe this is all some cosmic attraction we have no control over. What do we even know about each other?"

His eyes narrowed as he considered her question. In a move that stole her breath, he swept her up, cradling her in his arms, and plopped down onto the sandy shoreline of Point No Point. "I *know* you'll want to see this," he said to her before turning his face skyward. "Come meet Elara."

"Um, who did you call? Nothing is happening other than die-hard beachgoers leaving."

"You're impatient, but it comes as no surprise." He laughed when she pinched him. "Wait, oh, patienceless one."

She grinned at his playfulness. It hadn't come as a surprise either. What did was the knowledge that she remembered his easy laughter and engaging sense of humor, both from recent years and the past.

The first blast of air stole her wits. With the second, she squealed.

Whales!

And not any old whales, but *orcas*!

Her favorite species.

"How did you know? I've never said a word to anyone."

"You didn't have to. The snow globes on your shelves told me."

He shifted, positioning her back to his front, and pointed. "Look there."

A calf emerged from the water, assisted by its mother, and Elara caught her breath at the spectacular sight.

"I hope it survives. They don't always, and their first year is always iffy."

"Me, too. Why not give her added vitality?" he suggested.

"We can do that?"

"You can. Water nymph, remember?"

He laughed when she lunged to her feet and raced for the water. Halting, she spun back and pressed her hands to her chest. "Does this mean I can swim with them?"

"It does, but never let another human see you, and don't forget to warm your cells so you don't get hypothermia."

"Oh, Tripp!"

"Have fun, flitter-mouse."

She stopped skipping backward. "What about you?"

"This is your experience, Elara. Not mine."

"But what if I want to share it with you?" she asked softly.

Whipping his sweater over his head, he exposed his sculpted torso. Yes, all those defined ridges along his abdomen were drool-worthy, but it was those glorious, glorious shoulders that she longed to touch.

Then, he removed his pants.

"Holy shitballs!" She ran forward and jumped into his outstretched arms, climbing and clinging to him like a koala on bamboo. "Pass the salami!"

He laughed, and as he carried her to the water, her magical shoes morphed again, transforming into purple flippers.

"Ohmygawd! He's thought of everything!" she said.

"Yeah, he's annoying like that."

She giggled at the pique in Tripp's tone.

The joy she experienced interacting with orcas was something she'd never forget. They were respectful of the whales throughout the swim, making sure to convey good intentions through their energy. The pod accepted them, recognizing their supernatural status.

When the mother nudged the calf toward Elara, she thought her heart would burst. Visualizing a long, healthy life for the beautiful baby, she activated her nymph cells and rubbed her fingertips along its body. The pod formed a circle around them, balancing vertically in the water, their flukes down and their rostrums to the sky. It felt ceremonial, as if they were protecting her and the calf while she boosted the baby's vitality. She repeated the process for the mother.

As soon as they finished, the pod's matriarch offered her dorsal fin to surf Elara and Tripp toward the shore.

And that experience was all thanks to one person.

Tripp Nightshade.

CHAPTER TWENTY-SIX

That night, as Elara slept, she dreamed of her future, and Tripp was beside her. The vision gave her hope, and when she woke, it was with a fresh perspective, determination to find her parents, and a solid plan.

Tripp once again came through for her and presented a container of fire-bellied toad turds along with a morning latte.

"Gods, I love you!" she sighed after the first sip.

"You should. I spent the entire night looking for those little turds."

She giggled. The image of him hunting up the toads and waiting for them to poop was freaking hilarious.

"Laugh it up, buttercup, but you owe me."

"And I'll pay up," she promised. "*After* we've soothed the savage beast, or in this case, volcano."

"Don't think I won't hold you to it," he warned, but there was laughter in his incredible eyes, and she wished she could get lost there rather than do what she had to.

"We need a location large enough to cast a circle. I think it will have to be either the back room of *Wily Witches* or the bookstore's attic," he said.

If Elara had a choice, she'd go with the coffeehouse. "I'm not sure I should tell Flo. I don't want to open old wounds."

"I'll call the owner and see what I can arrange."

That had been two hours ago, and the scrying spell had been surprisingly easy. It had only required a pin-prick of her blood.

Now, here she was, standing with Tripp and accepting his comforting touch as she gazed at an impressive twenty-million-dollar beach house perched atop the three-story high natural dunes, with a single sandy path leading to the beach.

Her parents' home.

They'd teleported twenty minutes ago, yet she was locked in place, unable to find the courage to confront them. The two individuals who should've been her staunchest supporters. Who should've fought to keep their small family together, whatever it took. But who didn't care enough to.

The outside of their home was decorated with twinkling white LED lights and Christmas decorations in varying shades of teal. Beach-themed ornaments lined the silver garland.

Elara wanted to rip the freaking legs off the fake, bleached-out starfish and crack open the plaster sand dollars. Payton would have.

"My parents are in there," she said for what felt like the hundredth time. Her throat felt thick and scratchy. She'd dug into online records after she'd located them, searching for anything to indicate she had the correct couple. They'd lived here for the past seven years and, with their money, could've easily found Payton and her. It wasn't as if she and her sister had cloaked themselves as their parents had.

"I'm sorry," Tripp said.

"For what? That my parents are selfish pricks?"

He kissed her temple. "Let's hear their side of the story, flittermouse. Then you can shishkabob them over the open flames of Rainier if you want."

Despite her gut-churning dread, she laughed. "That had better not be your calming influence at play, mister!"

"Nope. It's my common sense and level head."

His sparkling, dark eyes glowed with love as he met her searching gaze. It had been this way since their shared experience with the orcas, and theirs was a bond never to be broken.

"We only have today to discover the last three things the boots require," she said. "We know this is one, but I can't figure out the other two."

"How about we scratch this off our list and clear our minds for whatever's left," he suggested.

"Good plan." Inhaling a steadying breath, she considered the best way to introduce herself to people who hadn't seen her since childhood. "What if they don't recognize me? What if they don't care?"

"It's doubtful your appearance has changed to the point they won't, and if they don't care, fuck them. You'll ask questions, demand answers, and say what you need to. The rest is, as they say, a bow on top."

"Fitting, considering Christmas is next week."

"I thought so," he quipped with a wink.

"Your resemblance to Hermes is pronounced when you do that."

Tripp dropped her hand. "That's it. I'm out."

Laughing, she chased him as he dodged to and fro.

"I'm sorry, you beautiful demigod!" she called out, too out of breath to play anymore. "I didn't mean it and won't ever repeat it. You're way hotter than Hermes."

Tripp pretended to consider her apology, then shrugged. "You're forgiven."

He caught her around the waist with one of those steely bands he called arms, swung her in an arch, and deposited her in the sand facing the ocean before kissing her.

"Dip your toes in the water, flitter-mouse. Recharge."

"Yesterday, I worried if we knew each other well enough. Now, I fear you know me too well."

"I merely see you as you are."

"A hot mess?"

He laughed. "A little of that, but mostly as a woman trying to save her hometown and the people who have come to mean a lot to her."

"I love you so much," she said, fierce and proud she'd come far enough to voice her feelings. "So damned much."

His grin practically melted her clothes right off.

"Okay, new plan." She gripped his hands in hers and placed them on her butt. "We go back to your apartment and play 'Pass me the salami.'"

His unrestrained laughter warmed her heart.

And she opened her mouth to tell him when a voice from behind him said, "I hate to break up a poignant moment such as this, but—"

Elara screamed, sending Tripp over the cliff to hilarity. He hugged his stomach and brayed like a jackass. Having had enough of his laughter at her expense, she hooked a leg behind his and shoved him. His tumble onto the sand didn't shut him up, and she shot the newcomer an exasperated glance.

"I'm sorry. He's—" Shock closed her throat.

"Hello, Elara," her father said with a broad, loving smile. Beside him was her mother, looking as serene and beautiful as ever.

A golden couple, with their stunning good looks and light, shining eyes.

For the briefest of moments, she hated them. Never had she allowed herself to feel such an ugly emotion, and she'd been the voice of reason during Payton's fiery rants. But seeing them standing there, without a care in the world and gazing upon her as if they had a right to be proud as punch, helped her understand her sister's constant rage.

She'd drown them in the ocean behind her if she didn't have a town to save and cursed boots to get the hell off her feet.

"Water, love," Tripp said, capturing her hand and tugging her away. "Recharge and center yourself, or this will end badly."

"Why do you say that?"

"The acidic purple air swirling around you."

She glanced up. "Remind me to kick Hermes in the balls before I take off these boots. Maybe the pointy end will hurt that shitbag."

"Count on it. I'll take pleasure in his pain."

"This is why I adore you, Tripp Nightshade," she said, stroking her fingers along his jaw. "Thank you for being my staunch supporter."

"Always, flitter-mouse."

"Tripp Nightshade?" Her father's expression became wary. "As in Enguerrand Nightshade and Brelenia of Messia's son?"

Elara snorted and addressed Tripp, "I think we gave them a reason to bolt again, don't you?"

"Give them a chance," he urged. To her parents, he said, "We'll be back shortly. Elara needs to replenish her water supply."

"You make me sound like a fish tank," she complained as they trudged to the water's edge.

"If the artificial coral fan fits…"

"I take it all back." She smacked his arm. "Hermes is the hotter one."

Tripp laughed, grabbed her by the waist, and ran with her into the crashing waves.

Twenty minutes later, they were dried off and sipping tea on her parents' balcony overlooking the Pacific. Tripp admired the view. Oddly, it reminded him of Messia, though the climate was vastly different.

"You have a lovely home, Mrs. Hawthorne," he said politely.

"Thank you." Mae was equally polite, but her smile bordered on dismissive.

"You look well, Elara," she said. She shot a curious glance at him. "I'm surprised to see you two together, though."

"Why? I'm not lovable enough? Not attractive enough for a demigod?" Elara asked.

Yes, she was chock-full of attitude, but she had to be damned tired of people dismissing her.

Tripp certainly was.

He had experienced something similar when he was her age. As the son of a wily Goddess, he was tested frequently. And as the years passed, he'd proved his mettle, but Elara would have to do double the work to prove her worth. Regardless of intelligence, a woman had to have twice the resilience and fortitude. Tripp hated it, but in society's eyes, it was still a man's world.

"That's not what I meant." Mae touched her wrist. "You seem like opposites. You're bookish, and he's—"

"Bookish," Tripp stated coolly. Why did everyone find it difficult to believe he could be attracted to Elara? She was intelligent, beautiful in her subdued way, and caring of everyone. "It's one of many things we have in common. I have a weekly standing order at the *Never Too Many* bookstore."

"My mother's shop." Mae's eyes misted. "How is she?"

"You'd know if you ever visited," Elara snapped.

Mae sucked in a sharp breath.

Rupert leaned in, his expression forbidding. "Don't speak to her that way, young lady!"

"What's this to be, then, Dad? A clash of the Titans?" Elara sneered. "I can tell by your surprise that you didn't think Payton or I would find out what we are."

His aquamarine eyes narrowed on Tripp. "Was this your doing?"

"Partially, but it wasn't intentional." He covered her balled fist with his hand. "Your daughter's magic was enhanced by a Trickster's, and the result woke her sleeping Titan and nymph cells."

Mae pressed her hand flat against her chest as if shocked. Perhaps she was. Or she was the best actress alive. If her distress was a performance, it was highly believable.

Rupert surged to his feet, rattling the china tea set and serving dishes.

"If this is true, and you've transitioned, you can't be here, Elara," he said. "It's not safe if your power has been activated." To Tripp, he said, "Find a secluded place for her—off grid—and cloak it. For her safety."

"Why are you acting like what I am is a horrible thing? Are you afraid all your bastard children will find you?" Elara taunted.

"Oh, Elara," her mother cried. "You have no idea."

"Then explain it to me."

"There's no time. You did a bad thing coming here, Elara," Rupert said, but his scolding tone was at odds with the longing in his expression. Here was a man who loved his daughter, but in her pain, she couldn't see it.

"Quickly, sir. Tell us what you know."

"No. Go back to where you came from. Back to…"

"Witchmere," Elara supplied dully.

"Go back to Witchmere, Elara, and when it's safe, I promise you I'll be in touch," Rupert said, placing a hand on Mae's elbow.

She jumped up, flung her arms out, and gestured to the sprawling three-story mansion. "And this is safe? A luxurious house on the coast, where anyone can find you? Give me a fucking break."

Her parents remained tight-lipped and silent.

She'd get no more from them. Her disillusionment was heavy, and Tripp sensed her pain. Secretly, she'd hoped for a reconciliation but was crushed when she didn't get it. He'd find a way to make it up to her.

After he climbed to his feet, he wrapped her in a tight embrace. Over her head, he met Rupert's haunted eyes. "Twenty-four hours is all we have left to stop a catastrophic event. If you wish to save your daughters"—he nodded to Mae—"and your mother, return there. Soon."

The dead-eyed stare Elara cast her parents chilled Tripp to his core. "Hundreds of thousands are at risk. Including those people you know and profess to care about. I won't say it's your *family* because you have none. Family doesn't do what the two of you did."

"Elara!" Mae gripped her husband's arm. "Rupert! Do something!"

"Rupert," Elara scoffed. "It's not even his real name." To Tripp, she said, "I'm going home to evacuate Witchmere if I can. You should go back to Messia. Please, save yourself."

"No, flitter-mouse. If you intend to be at ground zero for the blast, I'll stand beside you, holding your hand and looking into those gorgeous eyes. Your face is the last I want to see."

Her face contorted in an effort not to cry, and he offered his waiting arms as comfort.

"Let's go home, Tripp."

CHAPTER TWENTY-SEVEN

They walked the abandoned streets of Witchmere in disbelief. Shops were closed, and residents all appeared to have skedaddled in the short time they'd been gone. Tripp sent out feelers to check for others, but there were no life forces in the immediate vicinity.

"What do you suppose happened?" Elara asked, turning in a slow circle. "Where did everybody go?"

"Not sure. If I had to guess, I'd say Hermes and my mother were responsible for evacuating the residents."

"But he said a max exodus was too dangerous." She frowned and strode toward *Never Too Many*. "Don't you find it odd that Payton and my grandmother are gone? Or Archer, who Brelenia said was the town's protector?"

He did.

Cocking his head, he listened for sounds of wildlife.

Nothing.

"Elara, did you have any particular thoughts as we traveled back?"

"Not really." She frowned. "I might've wished you and I could live in a beautiful bubble away from everyone else's bullshit."

Of course! Her wish had overrode his simple teleportation spell.

"Your abilities are stronger than mine," he said. "You've isolated the two of us from the rest of the world."

"*I* did that?"

The shock in her voice was priceless, and Tripp wondered, not for the first time, what it must be like to experience the wonders of burgeoning magic. He'd been born with his and had fine-tuned it throughout life. Hell, he was still learning new tricks, thanks to Hermes. But going from the bare minimum to being the most formidable person in town had to be bizarre.

"Not to sound condescending, but I'm proud of you." He tugged a lock of her hair and conjured a beanie to cover her exposed ears. "You're mastering magic faster than anyone I've ever known and doing it in a way that doesn't create chaos for others."

"Minus the active volcano," she said dryly.

"Not your fault. That one's on my mother and Hermes."

"Agreed. But would we have realized we loved each other without this situation?"

"Yes." He led her to a bench, dusted it off, and drew her beside him. Twisting to face her, he toyed with her fingers and noted the size for when he proposed. "If you recall, I'd followed you home from Harrison's office."

"Because you thought I was upset by seeing you and Rowan."

He grinned. "You were."

"Meh." But she grinned back at him.

"Seeing the raw hurt in your eyes nearly destroyed me."

Elara frowned. "I thought I did a good job hiding what I felt."

"You do a great job of it for anyone who doesn't know you," he lied. "But I've made a job of studying you over the last two and a half years. I know your every expression."

"Creepy," she teased.

"No creepier than you ogling my shoulders," he retorted with a laugh.

"Busted. In fairness to me, they're splendid." She sighed wistfully as if imagining them naked.

His body reacted immediately, but he didn't act on it. This intimate moment was too precious to destroy with sex.

"It's the water nymph in you," Tripp said. "You're attracted to strong swimmers."

Her skin was the color of a ripe strawberry as she giggled.

"What did I say?" he asked, smiling and appreciating her charming amusement.

"Strong swimmers. That's a term for sperm."

"Ah." He grinned. "I have those, too, but we'll find a way to corral them so you don't wind up pregnant."

"You really wouldn't mind not having children? It seemed to be a deal breaker for your mom."

He mulled it over, trying to determine whether he wanted to carry on the Nightshade line. Elara's uncertainty was bothersome. "Your worth is more than a vessel for children, flitter-mouse." Tripp touched the area above her left breast. "Your heart is your true worth. It's open and generous."

"Not like yours."

"Much more than mine." He caressed the chilled skin of her neck, giving her a boost of warmth. "Even now, you're worried about my feelings or my mother's."

"But I don't want to tie you down only to have you resent me later."

"If we make it through the Trickster's test, we have centuries of love ahead of us." Leaning in, he planted a tender kiss on her tempting lips. "I love you, Elara. You. The soul that reincarnates, calling to me every lifetime, and is my perfect mate. I care not about the trappings of man or the need to procreate." He kissed her again. "I only want you beside me every day. The first face I see when I wake, and the last I see when I close my eyes."

"And I want you."

"You've made me the happiest man in the world," he said, meaning every word.

Her expression remained troubled.

"Why don't you want children?" he asked, determined to peel back the layers. "This isn't me pushing or attempting to change your mind. I want to know why you're so adamant about it."

"What if I turn out like my parents? What if, after I have kids, I grow bored and abandon them?"

"*That* is your fear?" he scoffed. Her scowl alerted him to the fact that he'd fucked up. "I wasn't making light of it. It's shocking that you believe you'd be a terrible mother. You look after everyone, Elara. You aren't the type to grow bored and abandon anyone. If that were the case, you'd have left Payton to her own devices years ago." Smiling at her confused expression, he said, "You also would've left Florence's grumpy ass to pursue your happiness. But once again, that soft heart of yours kept you rooted."

"I needed the money," she retorted.

"You have a trust fund worth a million dollars," he countered.

"One I won't touch. I don't want their guilt money."

"If you recall, Florence set those trusts up for you and Payton. Not your parents."

"Guilt money on her part, too," she said sourly.

"No. She needed to know you wouldn't struggle. She wanted you to have options."

Elara shifted to view the bookstore. "How do you know that?"

"I listen."

"I listen!" Her tone was offended.

"You do, but not regarding Florence or topics revolving around rejection." He held up a hand when she would've protested. "You've been hurt and have abandonment issues, flitter-mouse. And when someone mentions anything regarding it, you erect walls and become stubborn. It's a natural reaction."

"You think I'm being too hard on Flo?"

"Maybe. Maybe not. But knowing what you do of her after the years you've spent here, hearing the sage advice she's given, do you truly believe she doesn't care?"

Her silence stretched out as she stared at the bookstore, but Tripp didn't seek to intrude on her thoughts. In due course, she'd come to her own conclusions and realize Florence Shaw, while crusty and seemingly unfeeling, was a marshmallow when it came to her "gels."

"I owe her an apology, don't I?"

He held his thumb and index finger about an inch apart. "Maybe a small one."

Elara laughed and sandwiched his face between her palms. "Maybe you should've been my therapist instead of Harrison."

"But then we'd have had that whole doctor-patient taboo thing," he teased.

"Hmm. But I like the idea of taboo."

He pretended outrage. "Elara Elizabeth Hawthorne! Are you saying you're lusting after the buttoned-up Doctor Cobb?"

Laughing, she straddled his lap. "No, Tripp Nightshade. I'm saying I like the idea of playing doctor with you."

He conjured a lab coat with a snap. "Are you a naughty nurse or an improper patient I can't keep my hands off of?"

"Let's go with the improper patient. Then we can swap, and you can be the naughty nurse."

"If I've never told you before, I love your wicked streak."

"I didn't have one before the boots," she admitted.

He snorted. "Nonsense. You weren't wearing those blasted things when you wanted me to pass the salami in the alley last week."

Elara laughed. As she leaned in to show him exactly how wicked she could be, an explosion knocked her sideways into the snow.

"What the—"

Tripp hauled her to her feet and positioned himself in front of her to confront the threat.

They were both stunned stupid when her father spoke.

"I won't let you use my little girl, Nightshade," Rupert growled. "Step away from her, and I'll let you live."

No one was more surprised than Elara when Mae approached and called up the snow, turning it into a building-sized water spout.

"*We* won't let you use *our* little girl," she corrected.

"What the hell are you talking about? Have you gone crazy?" Elara screeched.

The ground rumbled, and she noticed the shimmering bubble encasing them for the first time. It rippled and dipped but held firm.

Tripp placed a hand on her arm. "Stay calm if you can. Remember the boots and Rainier."

"Got it. Thanks." Stepping around him, she placed herself between him and her parents. "I don't know what you have against Tripp, but I love him. You'll have to accept that he's my chosen mate."

A stone flickered on her boots, indicating she was on the right track.

But what exactly did they require?

"You left Payton and me to fend for ourselves with some half-baked hippie at a commune," she said, keeping the judgment out of her voice. "It hurt both of us to know we meant nothing to you." The purple beam flickered faster. She was getting somewhere! Curbing her excitement, she poured out her heart, keeping her angst at bay. "We had no knowledge of who you were or what we are, and had Tripp not uncovered our heritage, I might've died during the transition."

Her mother's gaze touched on him. "We were just in his apartment, Elara. He has a dossier on everyone in this town."

"Meaning he didn't just uncover what you were. He's known all along," her father stated grimly. "He's been playing you."

Doubts crept in, and the stone dulled as if it were being snuffed out.

Stepping forward, Tripp held out a hand to her. "Human lie detector, remember?"

She grinned and nodded. "I don't need to ask. I trust you."

"You shouldn't. He's a—"

"I know what he is, Dad. He's the man I love, and the man who loves me. We're not playing the games of the Gods or out to trick each other." She entwined her fingers with Tripp's, squeezing tightly. "He told me about his research. But consider this…"

Kissing his knuckles, she released him to approach her father. "Consider that he's a demigod who craves normalcy, not war. A man who feels the call of his mate's soul across time and space. One who is compelled to find her in each lifetime." She half turned and smiled at him. The fierce love in his glowing eyes made her entire body tingle. "One who values her thoughts and honors her by considering her feelings first, even if they are at odds with his."

"A man who would kill for her without question," he said gruffly. "But who would also make peace with a Titan determined to destroy him if it meant he could spend eternity with his mate."

"Why the files?" Her mother asked. The accusation in her voice had turned to curiosity. "What does it serve?"

"I've been on the run from a matchmaking mama for centuries," he said with a self-deprecating laugh. "Wherever I go, I learn the layout and look for those who might wish me harm. Those files give me an idea of who to watch out for. That's all."

"I don't buy it," Rupert snapped. "Elara's file is the thickest."

"Because she's the one I became obsessed with from the moment I set foot in Witchmere," Tripp confessed. "And I suspected the nymph heritage, but not the Titan. I found very little information on either you or Mae, Hawthorne."

"But your notes indicate you suspected her potential power. Do you deny it?"

A sick feeling started in Elara's stomach. The question was valid, and Tripp's guilty expression was damning.

He locked gazes with her. "No. I don't deny it."

CHAPTER TWENTY-EIGHT

"Why?" Elara asked.

Her suspicions were stirred, and Tripp's gut clenched. He had no good reason for digging deeper into her life.

"I don't know. Perhaps it was my obsessive need to discover everything about you," he said. "I truly don't know, flitter-mouse. Not any more than I knew to come to Witchmere, following the trail of your spirit's essence."

With a thoughtful frown, she held out her hand, and he placed his in hers, palm to palm. "Tell me the truth," she said.

The compulsion was more than he could bear, and he repeated everything he'd said to this point.

"Is there anything you haven't told me about your investigation or why you chose me?"

"No."

Shifting her grasp, she squeezed his hand. "I'm satisfied it's the truth."

"I'm not," Rupert snapped. "You're not thinking straight, Elara. You're thinking with your—"

"Careful," Tripp warned, refusing to let anyone insult her.

"I intended to say 'heart, not head,'" the Titan said, but his anger had lessened. Summing him up, Rupert asked, "You do realize I'm more powerful than you, son, yes?"

"I do."

"And still, you would stand up to me to defend Elara's honor?"

"I would."

Her parents shared a speaking glance.

"All right. We accept you as her protector."

Elara, ever contrary, scowled. "What? You can't make a declaration and expect everyone to bow to your demands."

Tripp laughed and caught her as she stomped by him. Swinging her around, he touched his forehead to hers. "He's not demanding I be your mate, flitter-mouse. He's accepting your choice and giving his blessing."

Though her scowl eased, she still wasn't thrilled. "I don't need anyone to accept my choices. They're mine."

"I won't disagree." He kissed the tip of her nose. "You and I will always make our own decisions."

"Always." Wrapping her arms around his neck, she tugged his head down until their lips were a whisper apart. "You're mine, and I'm yours."

"Always," he agreed, sealing it with a kiss.

When they parted, one of the two boot jewels they'd been unable to label shone brightly.

"Elara, look!"

Her cry of excitement was contagious, and he laughingly swung her around. "Only one more to go!"

"What's this?" Mae's confusion was endearing, and they took pity on her to explain. When they were finished, she tucked her arm through Elara's. "You've named all but the one, and the stone matching your relationship with us is still in flux. What can we do to help?"

The light turned solid.

"I think you just did, Mom," Elara said in awe.

"Splendid! Let's have tea."

Tripp remained behind as Mae led Elara toward *Wily Witches*.

Rupert hung back, too. "It's time we talked, Nightshade."

"No, sir. There will be time after we remove the last threat to Witchmere. Until then, we work together to help Elara."

"That's what I intended to say. But I was also going to say that I believe that last stone is yours, not hers."

"Why? Those bloody boots have been about her unresolved issues."

"Until now," Rupert replied. "You were too busy to notice, but the amethyst only lit when you committed to Elara."

"I committed when I told her I loved her," Tripp said. "My intentions haven't changed."

"Well, something happened between then and now. I know what I saw."

If it was true, then there was something he and Elara were missing in all of this. Something Hermes might clarify. But the Divine Trickster's cooperation was never guaranteed.

"What was it you wanted?" Rupert asked. When Tripp glanced at him in surprise, the man laughed. "I've been around a helluva lot longer than you, son. I know a troubled mind when I see one."

"I don't want her hurt when you and your wife leave again."

Rupert's eyes touched on his retreating family. "I doubt Mae will let that happen. She's been miserable far too long without her girls."

"Then why stay away?"

"I'm a Titan, Nightshade. You know what that means. Challenges by other gods because I'm the last of my kind."

"Until Elara."

Expression grim, the man nodded. "Until Elara."

A lead weight settled in Tripp's stomach. When word leaked of what she was, others would come to test her, hoping to steal her power.

"How have you survived until now? And why spend so many years in your beach house?"

"Both your questions can be answered the same way. We rarely stay there and are always on the move. It's just a place for Mae to replenish her magic."

"I see." And Tripp did. Maybe their town of supernaturals could band together and help him create a cloaking spell to protect Elara and, by extension, Payton. His mother might be willing if her ruffled feathers were soothed. Hermes might be on board, too. Tripp hadn't missed the caring in his cousin's eyes.

"What are you thinking?" Rupert asked.

"Just what it will take to protect her."

"If you aren't up for the task—"

"Fuck off. I'd lay my life down for her without question," he stated coldly. Lightning flashed. "Don't ever question my motives again, Hawthorne, or I won't be responsible for my actions."

Rupert surprised him when he grinned and slapped him on the back. The force behind the hit knocked him forward.

"I think you're perfect for my daughter, son."

"Thanks," he said, tone drier than dirt. "I have the feeling my life is about to get a thousand times more interesting with you and Mae around."

"Titans attract trouble. What is it the young'uns say? Sorry for your bad luck."

Tripp laughed. How could he not? In Rupert, he saw flashes of Elara's humor and grit. He'd be hard-pressed not to like the guy.

"Spill your guts, cousin."

Hermes glanced up to see Tripp bearing down on him. He had to hand it to the man; he was relentless regarding Elara's happiness and the safety of Witchmere.

"You should be excited, Tripp. There's only one stone left."

"Rupert Hawthorne suggested it might be my issue, not Elara's, and it got me thinking."

"Yes, I thought I smelled smoke. Silly me, I believed it was the ash," Hermes replied. Why not, when Tripp had set himself up for the dig?

"Do you *want* a broken nose?"

Tripp's visage lacked humor, and it wasn't hard to tell his patience was at an end.

Tired of the game and worried about how close they were to complete annihilation, Hermes sighed and said, "Yes, Tripp. The final one is for you. Happy?"

"I'd be happy to drop those fucking boots in the volcano."

"It's highly probable something—or someone—else should go in," he said lightly, providing the last clue.

Tripp inhaled sharply and failed to exhale.

"Breathe, man. You're already mush-minded. We can't have you lightheaded, too."

The enraged reaction was expected, but the strength behind his cousin's rage was a surprise. Hermes's head snapped back with the first blow to his jaw.

Wrapping his iron fist in Hermes's sweater, Tripp shook him like a mangy mutt with a bone. "If anything happens to Elara, I'll kill you.

"For the love of the Olympus! Get a hold of yourself, you animal! This is a two-thousand-dollar cashmere," he scolded, slapping Tripp's wrist. "And what do you take me for, anyway? I adore that adorable little sea urchin. Of course nothing is going to happen to her. Not if you get your head out of your ass."

After releasing him, Tripp sank onto the nearest chair and dropped his head in his hands. "How much time do I have?"

"Three hours."

"Gods, I hate you. Why did you do this to her?"

"Her? Not you?" Hermes asked.

"Of course not me. I've been around longer than anyone has a right to be, but Elara, she's never made it past thirty-five. How is that fair? Why shouldn't she be allowed to grow old and have a full, beautiful life?"

"Why, indeed." He wanted to tell Tripp he was close, but Trickster magic transformed over time. The last three hundred and fifty-plus years had made it unstoppable, giving the boots life. "You can sit here feeling sorry for yourself, or you can get your ass up to the summit. You know what to do."

"You said commitment. But what you meant was a personal sacrifice, wasn't it?" Tripp asked roughly.

"Yes."

"Fucking fantastic. I'll leave it for you to explain to Mother why her firstborn son dove into a crater of lava."

Hermes rolled his eyes. "Do you always have to be so dramatic?"

"Too bad I won't be around to see her strip the skin from your bones. I might enjoy that," Tripp taunted.

"Better get going. It's a long hike. I'll give Elara your love."

"You never quit, do you?" Tripp snarled.

"No, and neither should you."

CHAPTER TWENTY-NINE

"Tripp Nightshade!"

He whipped around to see Elara charging toward him.

"Stay there, flitter-mouse. The fumes are toxic, and with your body fresh from a transition, we don't know how it will react."

"What the hell do you think you're doing?" she demanded, and ignoring his suggestion to stop, she joined him on the summit. As she peered over the edge, she gripped his forearm, digging her nails in when she saw the bubbling lava. "Holy shitballs! Hermes said you intended to jump into the crater! Are you fucking insane?"

He almost laughed. Almost. Had the situation not been so dire, he might've. Fired-up Elara was his favorite, ranking right up there with Flustered Elara. With her cheeks flushed, eyes flashing, and fists clenched, she was prepared for battle, and it gave him a charge.

"I may be, yes," he said.

"There will be no jumping into the volcano. Do I make myself clear?"

"Elara—"

"No! I mean it, Tripp. We have two hours left. We can figure this out."

He gripped her shoulders. "Listen to me—"

"No!" Her sudden onslaught of tears nearly took him out at the knees. "No, Tripp. Two hours. There's still time. And look"—she pointed at the boots—"no light, so whatever you're doing isn't right."

"It won't light up until I go in." He hauled her close, confident he was correct. "Hermes all but said it."

"He's a fucking Trickster! He probably wants you boiled like a lobster before telling you you're wrong."

Tripp laughed, surprised he could.

Elara smiled, and it was the sweetest he'd ever seen. "Besides, when I offered to go in, he told me a sacrifice wasn't needed. He said, 'It wasn't as simple as that.'"

Tripp studied her earnest face. "Those were his exact words?"

"Yes."

What the hell was he missing? Hermes was a master at using innuendoes for clues, and he'd told Elara about Tripp's location for a reason. But what? The sulfuric fumes were getting to him, making it difficult to think.

Maybe the Trickster meant it wasn't as simple as Elara going in, but Tripp was the sacrifice? Hermes had confirmed it when Tripp asked about personal sacrifice.

"What is personal to me?" he asked her.

"What?"

"If I said I had to offer a personal sacrifice, what would you think I meant by it?"

"You would give up something or someone you love."

Her reply hit like a sledgehammer to the head. "Hermes is mad if he thinks I'd sacrifice you," he said savagely.

Elara paled.

In the next instant, her chin came up. "Do it."

"What?"

"Tripp, you have to do it. Toss me in."

"Fuck no! You're as crazy as he is if you think I will."

Lava arched up, splashing over the side of the crater, and Tripp barely managed to shift Elara in time to avoid her getting burned. He held her in a fierce embrace, unwilling to do what was necessary to save them and the town below.

She struggled against his hold, freeing herself enough to touch his face and gain his attention. "We have to try this. I'm dead either way."

Gazing up at him as she was, with her endearing face and wide blue eyes, Tripp recalled a popular Christmas cartoon. Without fail, he watched it every year, weirdly captivated by it since the day it aired. Now, he understood why. He couldn't prevent his grin.

"I just realized who you remind me of," he said.

Her brows met. "I remind you of someone?"

"Mmhmm." He glanced down the mountain toward Witchmere. The sun was setting, and holiday lights were barely visible in the distance. The scene resembled a real-life Whoville. "Cindy Lou Who."

"From the Grinch?" Her tone was a mixture of disbelief and amusement. "Why do I find it hard to imagine you watching a Jim Carrey movie?"

"No, not that one. The original animation."

"That makes more sense—not." She rolled her red-rimmed, bloodshot eyes.

"It does from my viewpoint," he assured her. "And it's understandable why his heart grew ten times that day."

"I was always in love with Max. He was so happy and adorable with his big eyes and single antler," she said with a melancholy smile. "I wanted a puppy just like him."

"If we had a future, I'd get you that puppy."

"I'd fall harder for you than I already have," she assured him. Sobering, she asked, "What now?"

"I have to try on the off chance it's me."

"Don't do it, Tripp. *Please*."

"A not-so-trustworthy source said it's what all the cool kids are doing these days."

She laughed through her tears and kissed him. "You're an idiot."

They were delaying the inevitable, but he didn't care. If she survived, she'd need memories of their lighthearted banter to see her through the hard times.

She leisurely trailed her fingers over the contours of his shoulders.

"You're only going to miss my glorious shoulders when I go."

"Glorious, glorious. They're worthy of the extra praise. Yours are the best I've seen." Smiling through her tears, she said, "I'll miss these desperately if you go."

"Makes sense. All water nymphs are attracted to men with broad shoulders."

"Really?" Pausing, she squinted up at him. "Are you making that up?"

"Nope. Probably a subliminal belief we're great swimmers."

"There you go with the sex talk again. Bragging about your swimmers."

He laughed. "I love you, Elara Elizabeth. Never doubt it, okay?"

"I know you do. I feel it here." Pressing a hand to her heart, she choked back a sob. "Maybe we go together? You fall, I fall."

"No. If this works, you deserve to live and love again."

"But I won't."

"You will, flitter-mouse. You're a Titan with centuries ahead of you. There's bound to be another gorgeous man with glorious, glorious shoulders." And Gods, did he hate the idea of her with another! But for her, he pasted on a smile.

"No dimples. You're being fake," she accused.

"It's because I don't want to imagine you with anyone else but me," he admitted with a genuine smile. "It makes me want to rip this mountain apart."

"Good. Jealousy is healthy in a relationship."

"It's not."

"You're not an expert. You couldn't even commit until yesterday."

He laughed. "I love how, in such severe circumstances, you maintain your humor."

"I'm told it's one of my most attractive qualities. That and my love of salami."

Tripp wasn't aware of sitting and clutching her tightly to his chest or of the tears freely flowing down his cheeks until she kissed them away.

"It's a damned good thing our location is exclusive," he choked out. "I'd be forced to hand in my man card if the other Gods saw me like this."

"True. I'd be forced to champion you," she agreed with a bittersweet smile. "But I'd do it. For you, Tripp Nightshade. You're worth everything."

She climbed to her feet, holding out her hand. "Come on. It's time to throw me into the volcano."

"You're cracked in the head if you think I'm going to."

From a short distance away, Hermes stood, cloaked and listening to the star-crossed lovers bicker about sacrificing themselves on the other's behalf.

"Don't be a shitbag. Light the last jewel already!"

"Ah, Stormy, my love! I see you're spying on me from your underwater lair," he said through their telepathic connection. "I was wondering when you'd interfere."

"She's my sister. Do you honestly believe I'd trust her welfare to anyone else?"

He chuckled. "I was counting on your protective instincts to kick in."

"Why?"

"So you'd talk to me again," he admitted. "I miss you."

"Gargle a nutsack, shitbag. This is for *her*, not you."

He laughed as he lit the stone. "And that is for *you*. Happy?"

"Pfft."

The silence grew, and if it weren't for the lightest buzzing in his ears, he'd have believed she'd disconnected.

"Thank you, Hermes."

"What can I say? I'm fond of the girl. She's got spunk. Like you." He rubbed the area over his heart, wishing things could be different and Storm could forgive him. But she'd held a grudge for over a century, and her stance hadn't softened.

"I'll grant you one more favor. But it better be a worthy one, nothing to do with sex when you're horny," she said.

Laughing, he nodded. "Duly noted."

There was another long pause before she said, "Do you think my father will stay in Witchmere this time?"

"Perhaps. He only left to protect Elara and Payton."

"So he says."

"So he says," Hermes repeated. "You should come here, Stormy."

"I'll think about it." And with that sassy reply, the buzzing in his ears stopped, severing their connection.

"I love you, Stormy," he whispered. "I always have."

The movement beneath them knocked Tripp and Elara to the ground. Layer after layer of earth piled on, killing the toxic smell and covering the river of lava prepared to erupt.

He almost rubbed his eyes in his disbelief.

"Tripp?"

"I see it, too."

"The stone?" she asked.

"No, the volcano went back to sleep." But he dragged his gaze away to look at her boots. "Thank Messia!"

"No, thank me," Hermes said, approaching in his cocksure, arrogant way. Tucked within the crook of one arm was a tiny black kitten. He handed it to Elara after Tripp helped her to her feet. "Hex 2.0."

Her china-blue eyes were liquid pools of love.

"Cindy Lou Who gets her Christmas after all," Tripp murmured.

Laughing, she rubbed her nose against the creature.

"Still want a Max?" he asked, stroking the kitten's dainty head.

"Absofreakinglutely!"

"No kids, but enough animals for a petting zoo?"

She grinned. "It's like you know me."

"Better than you can ever imagine," he agreed. Tripp offered a hand to Hermes. "I should break your pretty face, but I'm feeling a little euphoric at the moment."

"It's the sulfur. Your generosity will pass." Gesturing to the boots, Hermes said, "I'll need those back now."

"No! I earned them. Get yourself a different pair."

"Sorry, kid, but their return isn't up for debate."

Tripp eased the kitten from her grasp. "Please, for the love of Witchmere and my glorious, glorious shoulders, give him those fucking boots."

Sitting, she removed them, giving the fatal footwear one last hug and stroking the jewels. "Be kinder to the next owner," she said to the blasted things before handing them to Hermes.

Tripp fought a laugh and lost. "Snow's coming in. You'll need to conjure another pair, or your feet will freeze."

"Or I can climb on your back, and you can carry me home." She shot him a flirty smile. "It will give me time to admire your glorious, glorious shoulders."

Hermes worked a single lace free of its mooring and attached a multifaceted amethyst.

"Here, love. A gift to remember me by."

"Oh, I doubt I'll forget, but thank you." She held up the stone, admiring it in the fading light. "Who will get them next?"

"Not sure. They'll find their rightful owner after their magic is restored to full strength."

He leaned in and kissed her cheek. "Take care of yourself, love. If you need me, call out my name, and I'll be there." With a wicked glance at Tripp, he leaned closer to Elara. "But don't mistake us during sex and scream my name, or it might get awkward."

"Too bad the volcano isn't still active. I'd take great delight tossing you in," Tripp said dryly.

"That's my cue to leave." Hermes smiled down at the kitten. "That's one lucky p—"

"Hermes!"

"Keep your panties on, cousin. I was going to say 'pet.'"

Elara laughed and hugged him. "Sure you were. Get going, scoundrel."

EPILOGUE

Tripp Nightshade.

Elara sighed in contentment as he rolled onto his back and drew her close. "Did you feel the earth move? I'm sure I did."

"Don't even joke about it," he growled, giving her a one-armed squeeze.

"The ground or the sex?"

He laughed. "I was disappointed you didn't cry out, 'pass the salami,' when you came."

"It was a struggle to keep it in," she assured him, absently caressing one of his glorious, glorious shoulders. "I think you're right about the whole wood-nymph-broad-shoulder obsession. It's been a month of constant contact, and I can't stop touching them."

"Told you."

Smiling, she rolled atop him and rested her chin on her folded arms. "So, who do you think will get my boots next?"

"My balls just shriveled. Thanks for that."

Elara laughed.

"When you think about it, it wasn't so bad."

Tripp raised his head from the pillow and gave her an are-you-bonkers look. "For who? My cousin? Because from where I was sitting, it was a shit show."

"No, I mean it. No one got hurt, issues were resolved, my parents returned to Witchmere, and—best of all—you and I hooked up," she said. "I no longer have to duck into alleys to avoid you."

He laughed and rolled them over, settling himself between her thighs. "Now you duck into alleys to make out with me."

She grinned. "Isn't it great?"

"Did you have any doubt?"

"None."

As she gazed into his sparkling eyes, she sighed. How lucky could one girl be? "Thank you for always finding me."

"Thank you for always loving me."

"You're an easy man to love, Tripp Nightshade."

"Are you satisfied?"

Brelenia looked up from her ledgers as Rand entered their shared office. Granted, the space was one-half of an Olympic-sized swimming pool. "That's a loaded question, darling. Perhaps you should clarify."

"Tripp's happy and prepared to settle down." Rand perched on the edge of her desk and toyed with a snow globe Elara had gifted her. Inside was a miniature snow-capped Mount Rainier. "You should be over the moon."

"Oh, yes. The only thing that would please me more would be if she dismissed her ridiculous notions of modern women not having children."

"Brelenia." His tone was chiding, and it rankled.

"I know. I know," she said in disgust, directed mainly at herself and her inability to let it go. "I've heard it often enough from Tripp."

"Is it so bad?"

Brelenia shook her head. "No, and it isn't as if she doesn't have centuries to change her mind. I did."

"Yes, you did. It only took a millennia or two," he teased.

"It's hard work running a country, as you well know."

"Agreed." His grin was indulgent and loving. "But you do it admirably."

"I do."

"Which of our children is next on your list?"

"Not one of ours."

"No!" Rand surged to his feet and gripped the desk's edge. "You will not interfere with another mortal's life. I forbid it."

Raising a brow, she stared him down.

"Okay, so I don't necessarily forbid it. The Gods know *that's* impossible, but I'm begging you, Brel, please don't. Tripp and Elara barely averted disaster this time."

"Hermes and I have a failsafe in place."

"Impossible. It's Trickster magic for a pair of shoes dating back centuries. They have a life of their own." His features hardened. "Tell me this is not that blasted idiot's doing?"

She cast a glance over his shoulder in time to see Hermes enter.

"I'm offended," he said, looking highly amused as he approached.

Rand rounded on him. "As you should be, you dolt. You meddle in others' lives but can't manage your own relationships."

Pain flashed in Hermes's emerald eyes, but one had to be familiar with him to recognize it. With a careless shrug, he touched the snow globe, edging it closer to certain breakage.

Rand snatched it from Hermes and placed it on the desk's center. "You're worse than that blasted cat you pretended to be. Why must you toy with everything?"

A wicked gleam shone in her nephew's eyes as they locked with hers. "Because it's fun. Are you ready to discuss our next project, Brel?"

After throwing up his hands in defeat, Rand stalked to the sofa and plopped down, arms crossed and scowl firmly in place.

"Are you planning to stay for our meeting, darling?" she asked, already knowing damn well he wouldn't leave her alone with Hermes for fear they'd end the world.

His answer was a tight-lipped glare.

"Payton Hawthorne will be our next project," she declared.

Rand hung his head. "I should warn the girl."

"Don't you dare, or no sex for a decade!" Acting magnanimous, she gave a slight shrug and toyed with her pen. "But you can help steer the outcome if you'd like."

"You're a cruel, cruel woman, Brelenia of Messia, and you run a hard bargain."

She grinned. "You're in?"

"I'm in."

THE END

Thanks for reading Wicked Witchmas. I hope you thoroughly enjoyed my story. If so, please consider pre-ordering book two in the series, WANTON WITCHMAS, available through my webshop: https://tmcromer.shop.

Turn the page for a sneak peek!

Not ready to order? That's cool, too.
Sign up to be alerted when the book goes live:
http://subscribepage.io/wanton

WANTON WITCHMAS SNEAK PEEK

"You're under arrest."

A high-powered LED flashlight beam blinded her, making it impossible for Payton Hawthorne to see the uniformed officer intent on hauling her to the pokey.

But she recognized the voice. It had haunted her dreams for years.

Dailey Cobb.

Her ex-fiancé and the one that got away.

Or rather, the one she left standing at the altar.

Payton froze in place, unable to speak.

Her best friend and current partner in crime, Rowan Sanderson, had no such problem. "Listen, Officer Knob—"

"Cobb," he ground out.

"You sure?" Rowan squinted like she believed he was lying. "Because you're being a total knob—"

"Ro!" Payton cleared her throat. It was time to take back the reins of the situation. "Right. So, I know you probably hear this a lot, but it isn't what it looks like."

"You're right," he replied. "I hear it a lot."

He didn't lower the beam as he approached, and she raised a hand to shield her eyes. The unmistakable sound of handcuffs clinking as they cleared their holder was intimidating as hell.

"I'm pretty sure those are the exact words you used when I caught you sneaking out the window on our wedding day," he said coldly. "Now turn around. You're under arrest."

"Lee, please, you don't understand—"

"I don't want to, either. And my name is Officer Cobb to you, Hawthorne."

He moved into the ring of light provided by the overhead street lamp, looking for all the world like an avenging angel as the beam caught and highlighted his close-cropped golden hair.

Payton tamped down the regret.

Dailey Cobb's handsomeness hadn't faded in the three years since she initially bolted. If anything, he'd grown hotter. But those steel gray eyes were no longer molten silver when they looked at her. Instead, they were flat, resembling aged concrete in need of a good pressure wash, and except for a burning anger, those once-incredible, sparkling eyes were now dispassionate and bordered on lifeless.

She sensed the simmering rage underneath his cool, collected exterior, and it fucking cut that there was no forgiveness in him. But how much could she expect when she was always in the wrong?

With a worried glance at Rowan, Payton stepped backward and hid her hands behind her.

"You understand that's resisting arrest, don't you?" Dailey asked. "That's going to add more time to your sentence."

Why did he have to sound so gleeful at adding another charge to her B&E?

"Lee—" His thundercloud expression had her correcting her slip. "Uh, Officer Kno—Cobb! Officer *Cobb*... I, uh... that is to say, *we*... we're not breaking the law. This is all a misunderstanding concerning my sister's engagement party." She ended with a sigh and gave him a weak-ass smile. "So there's really no need to arrest us."

"Party? To be clear, you've been partying tonight?"

"Well, ye—er, no! No, not at all." But she had, and she was the worst liar on the planet. A fact he knew well.

"You'll have to take a breathalyzer."

Rowan ran.

With her long, auburn hair flying behind her like the flag of a retreating troop, she took off for the surrounding woods and never looked back. And damned if Deputy DoRight didn't let her go. Why not? His main goal was to make Payton's life a living hell ever since the day she decided to spare him from the misery of marriage to her.

"She always leaves you holding the bag," he said. "You have terrible taste in friends, Hawthorne."

"Her fight-or-flight instincts kicked in. It's the wolf thing. Also, being burned as a witch in a previous life makes her skittish around authority figures."

"Makes sense. Are we doing this the easy way or the hard way?"

She shouldn't have felt the thrill of his words down to her toes, but the low, suggestive way he spoke reminded her of the times they'd spent between the sheets. They'd never had a problem with sex. Their issues had stemmed outside the bedroom.

"It's Elara and Tripp's engagement party, Officer Cobb." Did she see a softening of his expression? She flattened her hand over his uniformed chest. "Will you just overlook this one, er, indiscretion?"

He stared into her beseeching eyes for the longest moment before his gaze dropped to her lips. "What are you proposing?"

Sensing success, she sidled closer. "What do you want?"

A wicked grin curled his mouth, and she experienced another zing. His voice was friendly, almost teasing, when he asked, "Are you offering me a bribe, Payton Hawthorne?"

"I suppose I am," she replied huskily, caught up in the nostalgia of being close to him again.

He lowered his head as if he were about to kiss her, but at the last second, he shifted, lifted a strand of her dark blonde hair to rub between his fingers, and whispered into the shell of her ear. "I'm adding attempting to bribe an officer to your charges."

His tone was so deep and sexy that she didn't at first register what he was saying. Yet the feel of the metal enclosing her wrist snapped her out of the sexual haze he so effortlessly wove.

Damned warlocks!

Payton jerked back, but it was too late. He'd already snapped the cuff in place and secured her opposite wrist within his large, unrelenting grip.

"Please, Lee," she whispered. "Please don't do this. Don't ruin Elara's night."

"I'm not ruining her night. You did that by driving under the influence, breaking and entering a business, resisting arrest, and bribing an officer of the law." His smile was smug, and she wanted to strike him. "Looks like you'll be spending a lot of time behind bars. That can't be easy for someone who prefers to run away rather than deal with her problems."

"What happened with us was more than dealing with a singular problem, and you damned well know it," she retorted.

"Right. You didn't want the commitment of marriage to *me*. The man who once loved you."

The man who once loved you.

Did she hear an emphasis on the word once? It had been years. She shouldn't still feel a pang whenever she thought of what they had, of what she'd impetuously thrown away.

"I didn't want the constant commitment of being ruled by your mother. The mayor of this podunk town," Payton stressed as if he didn't already know how much power his mother held.

Although his brows shot up, he appeared unmoved.

"You know that, but whatever." She lifted her cuffed arms. "Throw the book at me if it makes you feel like a big man."

"That's the thing, Payton. I haven't felt anything since you disappeared again last year. Not one goddamned thing except anger. And you're going to fix the curse you put on me before you run away this time."

"Curse?" Dumbfounded, she gaped. What the hell was he talking about? "What curse?"

BOOKS BY T.M. CROMER

Get your printable list here:
www.tmcromer.com/printable-booklist

PARANORMAL ROMANCE

These Boots Are Made For Witching Series:
WICKED WITCHMAS
WANTON WITCHMAS

The Thorne Witches Series:
SUMMER MAGIC
AUTUMN MAGIC
WINTER MAGIC
SPRING MAGIC
REKINDLED MAGIC
LONG LOST MAGIC
FOREVER MAGIC
ESSENTIAL MAGIC
MOONLIT MAGIC
ENCHANTED MAGIC
CELESTIAL MAGIC
EVERLASTING MAGIC
CAPTIVATING MAGIC
DISCOVERED MAGIC

The Thorne Witches: Happily Ever Afters Series:
ENDURING MAGIC
BOUNDLESS MAGIC

The Unlucky Charms Series:
PINTS & POTIONS
WHISKEY & WITCHES
BEER & BROOMSTICKS
COCKTAILS & CAULDRONS
WINE & WARLOCKS
HIGHBALLS & HEXES

The Sentinels of Magic Series:
THE AETHER
THE DEATH DEALER
*THE SEER
*THE TRAVELER

Angels of Legend Series:
*LUCIFER

CONTEMPORARY ROMANCE

The Holt Family Series:
GOODBYE TO YOU
THIS TIME YOU
INCLUDING YOU
A LIFE WITH YOU

Fiore Vineyard Series:
PICTURE THIS
RETURN HOME
ONE WISH

Stonebrooke Series:

BURNING RESOLUTION

HIDDEN RESOLUTION

* At the time of Wicked Witchmas's publication, these stories were still in the writing stage. Some can be found via a serial story app, but all are expected to be published by the end of 2025.

BIO & FOLLOW LINKS

T.M. Cromer is a multi-award-winning sorceress of the written word and fearless architect of high-stakes paranormal romance. With a flair for twisty plots, slow burns, and swaggering heroes hot enough to scorch the page, she conjures stories that hook readers and refuse to let go. From her cozy PNW lair, flanked by two Hellhounds and an unholy amount of caffeine ambition, she weaves love, danger, and humor into every page. Whether it's witches, sirens, or magical assassins, her characters never behave, and neither do her stories.

When she's not dreaming up new ways to ruin her characters' lives before crafting their HEA, she's daydreaming about swimming with orcas or cackling over a particularly clever line of dialogue. Come for the magic, stay for the heartbreak, and maybe fall a little too hard for a man who only exists on the page.

Want to stay current on what's happening in T.M. Cromer's world? Subscribe to her newsletter to receive release news and promo alerts.

You can also join her VIP reader group on Facebook to chat with her, participate in polls, and stay up-to-date on what's happening. Become a member today!

FOLLOW T.M. CROMER:

facebook.com/tmcromer
instagram.com/tmcromer
tiktok.com/@tmcromer
pinterest.com/tmcromer
amazon.com/stores/T.M.-Cromer/author/B011QK3WXY

www.ingramcontent.com/pod-product-compliance
Lightning Source LLC
LaVergne TN
LVHW010256260326
834688LV00044B/1313